The Cutt[ing Room]

"The Blade's got anothe[r one.]"
"Damn! Was she still ali[ve?]
Did she have a chance to say anything?"
"No way. You know how that sonuvabitch operates. Damn near cut her head clean off..."

Shockwaves

"Disturbingly subversive... Tessier knows no limits except those of his own considerable imagination, which is poetic and savage by turns, and always surprising."
—Ramsey Campbell

Also by Thomas Tessier from Berkley Books

Phantom

"Frightening... I won't be able to get the book or its characters out of my mind for weeks!"
—Peter Straub

"Chilling... terrifying!"
—*Library Journal*

"The tension rises like a frightful fever and peaks at nightmare!"
—*Publishers Weekly*

The Fates

"A good contemporary horror novel!"
—Karl Edward Wagner

Berkley Books by Thomas Tessier

Phantom
The Fates
Shockwaves

THOMAS TESSIER
SHOCK WAVES

B
BERKLEY BOOKS, NEW YORK

FOR CAROL SMITH

This Berkley book contains the complete
text of the original hardcover edition.
It has been completely reset in a typeface
designed for easy reading and was printed
from new film.

SHOCKWAVES

A Berkley Book/published by arrangement with
the author

PRINTING HISTORY
Severn House edition published 1983
Berkley edition/September 1987

All rights reserved.
Copyright © 1982 by CW Corporation.
This may not be reproduced in whole or in part,
by mimeograph or any other means, without permission.
For information address: The Berkley Publishing Group,
200 Madison Avenue, New York, NY 10016

ISBN: 0-425-09477-4

A BERKLEY BOOK ® TM 757,375
Berkley Books are published by The Berkley Publishing Group,
200 Madison Avenue, New York, NY 10016.
The name "BERKLEY" and the "B" logo
are trademarks belonging to Berkley Publishing Corporation.

PRINTED IN THE UNITED STATES OF AMERICA

10 9 8 7 6 5 4 3 2 1

PROLOGUE

◆

Old man Wooton's beat-up Mustang rattled over Twelve Mile Road, young Craig Wooton behind the wheel. It was shortly before two in the morning. On the radio, Donna Summer began to breathe heavily in stereo, interrupted every few seconds by a short burst of static. There was a storm in the air.

Bonnie Howe, the girl sulking on the passenger seat a foot away, was supposed to be home by two, according to her ridiculous father. Not that it mattered as far as Craig was concerned. Bonnie wasn't putting out yet, as he had discovered earlier that evening. They had gone to the local drive-in, which was showing *Dawn of the Dead* and *The Corpse Grinders*. Which, as it unfortunately turned out, they watched. Too bad. Bonnie was a cute kid. Nice build and only sixteen. Obviously he'd have to work on her. She had downed a couple of cans of beer and was a little tipsy, but it hadn't done him any good. She wouldn't even let Craig get his hand under her sweater. Maybe they're religious, he thought. Craig draped his right arm around Bonnie's shoulders, hoping to angle his hand down for another unsatisfactory feel.

'Craig.' Bonnie sighed histrionically.

'What?'

'Just drive, please.'

'I am, what does it look like I'm doing?'

She hadn't moved his arm away, but neither had she moved herself an inch closer to him. I can't believe it, he told himself. It's ridiculous. Now all I get to play with is her goddamn earring.

'Try driving with both hands,' Bonnie suggested. 'You know this road is bad, and the car sounds like it's about to fall apart.'

'My brother drove it into the ground,' Craig complained. 'I'm gonna buy my own. A big car with plenty of leg room front and back. With reclining seats.' Let's see what she says about that.

But then the news came on the radio.

'We're late,' Bonnie said unhappily. 'I'm gonna get killed.'

'Five more minutes,' Craig soothed, trying unsuccessfully to pull the girl closer. 'What's with your father anyway?'

'I have to be in by two o'clock,' Bonnie repeated as if she had been told it a million times.

'Ridiculous.' Craig unwrapped his arm, which had accomplished so little and was beginning to ache, and punched the radio to another station.

When he finally pulled the car up in front of Bonnie's house he almost thought his luck was changing. Maybe she had resigned herself to being in trouble for coming home a few minutes late, or maybe she got an extra kick out of necking right under her father's nose. Whatever it was, Craig found her saying good night very passionately. All right, he thought, this is more like it. He managed to get his hand under the back of her sweater and, a discreet yank later, under her blouse. Lovely, warm, smooth skin, sweet sixteen and another tent raised in his lap. But before Craig could get to her bra, Bonnie kissed him on the nose, backed away and reached for her purse.

'Hey, where are you going?' he asked forlornly.

'I'm in trouble already,' Bonnie replied. 'I don't want to make it any worse than it is.'

'Aw, hang on. You're back at the house, that's the main thing.'

'You don't know my father.'

'Okay.'

'When?'

'Next week-end?'

'Not till then?' This girl has promise, Craig was thinking. But she needs a quick combination of punches. A whole week in between was too long. 'How about tomorrow night, or Sunday?'

'I'll have to see what my father says. I'll be lucky to get out again before next week-end.' Bonnie started to open the car door. 'Thanks for the nice time.'

Yeah, nice. 'Hey, wait a minute.' Craig reached for her.

'I have to go.'

'I can't go like this,' he said, hoping, at the last moment, that she would notice and do something about the problem in his lap.

'Why not? What's the matter?'

'Hey, I like you,' Craig whispered, pulling her back to him. If only he could somehow nudge her hand down between his legs.

'I like you too,' Bonnie said earnestly. 'But I really have to go now. Phone me tomorrow.'

'Maybe you ought to wait a little longer to make sure he's asleep when you do go in,' Craig offered, feeling her breasts through the bulky sweater and blouse. Yeah, they were definitely worth extra effort.

'No, he usually waits for me to come in the door,' she fibbed. Anything to get away. Bonnie felt like she was trapped in a tin can with an octopus. 'I'm only a few minutes late, I can still make excuses. Call me tomorrow. Bye.' Then she was out of the car and trotting across the front lawn to the big, dark farmhouse.

Son of a bitch, Craig Wooton muttered, watching her snug fanny bounce away in farewell. That girl has promise, no doubt about it. But here I am driving home again with a loaded gun. They play you like a goddamn yoyo, up and down, up and down. What the hell can you do about it? He was getting tired of beating his meat—at seventeen, for Chrissake! Not even a dry hump at the passion pit, hell you would have thought at least that much. Is it the car? Shit, it could be any damn thing.

It would be different when he got to college, that's for sure. College girls love to screw. Once you got them away from home they'd do anything. Barry Sheedy had told him all about it, and Barry never even went to college. He just hung around with some college guys in Salt Lake City so he could get fixed up with dates. Yeah, it'd be better then. But college was still a year away ... Craig Wooton swung the car around and drove back over Twelve Mile Road towards home, the soft dashboard lights illuminating his disgusted features.

Inside, Bonnie closed the front door quietly and stood leaning against it for several seconds, letting her eyes adjust to the dark. She was grateful to find that her father wasn't waiting up, ready to explode, almost eager for her to be a minute late. But tonight he was sleeping and all she had to worry about was whether or not the old man had heard Craig's car arrive out front and then roar away. If that happened, her father would note the time on the luminous dial of his clock radio and fix it firmly in his mind for recall the following morning over breakfast. That, at least, wasn't quite so bad.

Bonnie moved away from the door and discovered that she was a little unsteady on her feet. The beer must have had more of an effect than she thought. Still, it hadn't prevented her from keeping Craig under control. He was all right, but like the others she had dated he was ready to jump on you at the first opportunity—even while waiting at a traffic light. Bonnie wasn't afraid of sex but she believed there was a right time and place for it. How could Craig even think of it in that cramped, grubby old car? Besides, it was only their first date and for Bonnie a first date was by definition not the right time for sex play. Unless, of course, it was a first date with Clint Eastwood.

Better take something before going to bed, she thought. Might ward off a hangover and make it easier for her to face her father in the morning. With careful, measured steps, Bonnie made her way to the bathroom, found a bottle of Bufferin and went into the kitchen. She didn't bother to turn on the overhead fluorescent light, which would be too harsh at this hour. She let the tap water run until it was good and cold, then washed down three Bufferin tablets. She felt better at once, the water rinsing away some of the stale beer taste in her mouth. She poured another glassful and went to sit down in the breakfast nook for a minute.

Even if she did get in trouble for coming back late it was nice to be up and awake at this time of day, Bonnie thought. So relaxing to sit alone and listen to the sounds of the house settling, the mountain wind playing through the trees outside. Early October. A good time of the year, a time when the season turns forcefully in Utah and the air is charged with last energies before the winter freeze arrives.

Bonnie heard the back porch door open and then click shut. A shadow moved on the far side of the kitchen.

'Ted, is that you?' she whispered, thinking it might be her older brother up for some reason. There was no answer, but then she could see it wasn't Ted; this person was taller, thinner. One of Ted's friends, Bonnie thought. Drunk probably, and a couple more of them waiting outside. It had happened before: they get tanked up and then have the brilliant idea of rousing Ted to join their little party. Bonnie wasn't worried. She was in her own home and she could handle this, no sweat. Better get rid of him before he wakes up Dad and there's really hell to pay.

'Come on,' Bonnie whispered urgently as she rose. 'Get out of here before I call my father. He'll kick your ass over the hill and gone.'

Only faint light came through the kitchen window. Bonnie didn't recognize the young man standing there and staring at her. Tall, fair-haired, with a friendly grin on his face. In his mid-twenties, maybe. He didn't seem drunk.

'Who are you and what are you doing here?' Bonnie asked without the slightest trace of fear.

'You're just the girl I've been looking for,' the stranger said, and before Bonnie could move, he leaned over and kissed her full on the mouth, warm and deep.

She was momentarily overwhelmed. If Craig Wooton could kiss like that, the evening might have been a lot more enjoyable. Trouble, trouble, her mind insisted, but she no longer seemed able to do anything about it.

'Hey, wait,' Bonnie gasped, trying to recover.

The young man's eyes caught what light there was and appeared to burn within. Bonnie tried to think, to say something, but she found it impossible to concentrate on anything but those eyes.

The stranger embraced her and as he kissed her, Bonnie felt exquisite pleasure flooding through her body. This is crazy, she thought, but she knew she was going to give herself to him, there and then, on the kitchen floor. It was all she could think of. But then something sharp and cold entered her flesh, cutting deeply into her, and a tiny cry died in her throat as Bonnie Howe was swept into darkness.

The tall, young stranger knelt over her, the same slightly sheepish grin still marking his face. Then he set to work.

1
♦
COURTSHIP

ONE

◆

Among the people who boarded the 3.10 train in New London that Friday afternoon were two students from Connecticut College. Jackie Pierce and Sandy Goddard hoisted their overnight bags up on to the luggage rack and then fell into their seats.

'Don't look so gloomy,' Sandy advised. 'You'll have a great time, wait and see. Just give it a chance.'

Sandy had made these week-end excursions several times before and had a 'kind of a relationship' with Dan Black, a Yale University law student. But this was Jackie's first Yale week-end and she was feeling uneasy about it.

'I met Stu the last time I was there,' Sandy went on. 'You'll like him.'

'What's his last name again?' Jackie asked unenthusiastically. She disliked blind dates.

'Shepard. His father's big in something in New York, I'm not sure what. But they have a lot of money.'

'I don't care about that.'

'I know, I know,' Sandy said hastily. 'I'm just telling you what I know about him, that's all.'

The girls lapsed into silence for a few minutes as the train proceeded west with a gentle, rocking movement. Jackie watched the trees fly past, a riot of dazzling autumn colours. The best time of the year, she thought.

'What's he studying?' Jackie asked finally.

'Law, same as Dan.'

That figures, Jackie thought. Good family name doing law at Yale. Destined to be well off. An ideal date, a lot of girls would think. So why was she feeling depressed? She wasn't afraid of meeting people, and certainly not of going out on dates. But there was something in her that wanted to hold back a little, some pocket of reserve she couldn't completely dismiss.

It had to do with Todd Jackson, of course. He had taught Jackie's first year English course last year. Tall, thin, incredibly pale, Jackson was a young pre-Raphaelite ghost of a poet. Half the girls at the college would have been glad to mother him and minister to his needs, and Jackie was one of those (there must have been others, she realized later) who did become involved with him. 'Jackie tender leaf', was what Todd called her. It lasted three months and was still an embarrassment to her sense of self-esteem.

What a foolish little girl she had been. Eighteen, breathless from high school, eager to enjoy life, to experience new things, to meet people, to learn, to discover Truth, Meaning, Love, Beauty . . . And so on. Todd, being a poet, had a direct pipeline to all of these things. He taught Jackie to be free and how to use that freedom, to be herself, to think and feel like a woman . . . Oh, it was all so preposterous and wrong, looking back on it now.

Jackie could hardly bear the thought of it, and yet it was something she feared she would never be able to forget. Todd Jackson, poet and perfect master. He had taught her, all right—to be his idea of a woman, to feel the way he wanted her to feel, to be absorbed in and devoted to what was important to him. To be his little slave. Then he dropped her. Just like that. Reality time, babe. You can't argue with poets. Thanks, Todd. You just kinda wasted my precious time.

But not entirely, Jackie knew. It was an experience, as they say, and maybe it was better for her to have gone through it when she did. It was over, out of the way, done. She had learned a thing or two, about other people but especially about herself. What she resented most was that reserve, that pocket of wariness that had formed within her and raised a red flag in the back of her mind every time she met another man. It's just one of those things, Sandy had said at the time. Part of growing up.

Jackie had quite enjoyed sex with Todd in the beginning—it was one of the things that made her memories so bittersweet. She had found it hard to accept that someone who was basically a nasty person had, at one time, made her feel so great physically. Later she realized that it wasn't Todd; it was really just herself, discovering the full power of sex for the first time. But sex could be dangerous, drawing you and holding you to someone when the rest of the relationship was turning bad, destructive. She had to be careful. Jackie couldn't let another man like Todd Jackson into her life, even if it meant leaving her sex life in limbo for a while. Some day, maybe, she thought wistfully, I'll walk into a good, healthy relationship, one that works on all levels for both people. Even if it doesn't last for ever, as long as it's good and honest, and doesn't leave an ugly feeling afterwards, that feeling of having been used, manipulated.

Oh Jackie, snap out of it, she scolded herself. What a way to start the week-end. They were going to dinner and a special lecture this evening, followed by a party, and tomorrow there was the Yale-Cornell football game, dinner and a dance. Sandy was right: relax and have a good time.

New Haven's train station is a shabby old brick building that stands as the last remnant of a neighbourhood that has long since been wiped out by highways and parking lots. But Dan and Stuart were there to greet the girls. Jackie had met Dan once before, when he visited Sandy in New London. He was a solid six-footer with the kind of reliable face and manner that could, in ten or fifteen years, sell life insurance on television. He dressed well, if conservatively, and had an air of quiet efficiency about him. A young man who knew where he was going and how to get there.

Stuart Shepard was about the same height as Dan, perhaps an inch shorter, and he wore a three-piece corduroy suit. He would wear the same suit tomorrow and Sunday when they saw the girls off at the train station, by which time Jackie was convinced that Stuart was born for three-piece corduroy suits. He was friendly and trying hard, so much so that after a few minutes Jackie found herself making an effort to put him at ease. She relaxed completely, seeing at once that however else the week-end went, she would have no problems with her slightly pedantic, well-meaning date. She might even enjoy herself.

The apartment the girls were to stay in comprised one large room, a galley kitchen and bathroom.

'The couch opens out into a second bed,' Dan explained when they arrived.

'We brought along some snacks and liquid refreshment for you,' Stuart added, setting down a large brown grocery bag on the table.

Dan poured the drinks while Stuart settled himself on the couch and did his best to be friendly and attentive.

'Tell me again where we're going tonight,' Jackie requested.

'A lecture,' Sandy said. 'But there's a party after it.'

'Brooks Matthews,' Stuart said. 'The lawyer.'

'Who's he?' Jackie asked.

Dan took control again. 'It isn't as bad as it sounds. Matthews is a good speaker and he should give an interesting talk. He's a district attorney in Utah and he's generally regarded as one of the best prosecutors in America. Handled some important cases.'

'The Judd Taylor case,' Stuart began.

'That made his name,' Dan continued authoritatively. 'But it was only because he was fresh out of law school at the time. It wasn't that important a case in legal terms.'

'True,' Stuart agreed. 'But it's still his most famous case.'

'Anyhow,' Sandy cut in. 'There's a party for this man after his lecture, and we're invited. Right?' She looked at Dan, who immediately nodded.

'Stuart and I are obliged to attend the talk, but I think you'll enjoy it too. Mr Matthews may be our President one day.'

'Here at Yale?' Jackie said.

'No. President of the United States.'

'You're kidding.' Jackie had never heard of Brooks Matthews until five minutes ago.

'He has a long way to go,' Stuart said.

'Yes, but we've had unlikely nominees before,' Dan explained. 'It's an open secret that Matthews intends to run for the Senate at the next election, and he seems certain to win it. Four years after that he'll have as good a shot as anybody at the Republican nomination. The party's always up for grabs and the fact that Republicans are talking about him already says a lot.'

Sandy chuckled. 'So we get to check him out early.'

They finished their drinks and went out for dinner. The conversation was pleasant and easy, the food good.

After dinner they walked across the Old Campus, which looked especially beautiful in the October dusk light. The meal and wine had apparently loosened

Stuart up and he chatted with Jackie all the way.

'What are you going to do after you get your degree?'

Jackie smiled to herself. The usual question, just took Stuart a little longer to get to it. 'I don't know,' she replied.

'Well, you've got plenty of time to decide. Don't commit yourself until you're really sure.'

'I want to do something,' Jackie said definitely. 'I'm studying history now but I don't want to teach.'

'There are any number of fields you can go into with a solid arts background. And it's easier for a woman to get a job these days than it is for a man.'

'Don't start that,' Jackie warned with a laugh.

Stuart rambled on with his comments and advice innocuously, but Jackie was only half listening. She really did want to do something with her life. There were dozens of possibilities, but when you're nineteen they all have a way of hanging in the air like big, unwieldy balloons. Pick this one, pick that one—how can you when you don't know what they're all about and would involve? And once you've made a choice you'd better be right: it's harder to change a career than it is to get a divorce.

'Another couple of minutes and we might not have found seats,' Stuart said. The lecture hall was nearly full.

'How long's this going to take?' Sandy asked.

'Wait and see.' Dan smiled.

At eight minutes past eight a professorial gentleman approached the podium and delivered the standard introductory speech. Applause greeted the guest from Utah.

Brooks Matthews stood and let his eyes roam over the audience before speaking, holding his silence long enough to be sure he had the complete attention of everyone in the place. Jackie was immediately impressed by the way the man looked. He must be six-three, she thought. His face had strong, almost rugged features. His hair was silvery and swept back to a judicious length, curling slightly at the back. He wore a blue velvet dinner suit which fitted him perfectly. He had real physical presence, and you couldn't avoid noticing it.

'Tonight we're going to talk about killing people,' Brooks Matthews started. 'Husbands killing wives, wives killing husbands, a stranger killing another stranger in a bar, a fourteen-year-old boy killing his parents as they lay sleeping in bed at night, or a policeman killing a suspected criminal. Killing people —premeditated or impulsive, cold-blooded or in a moment of passion. To kill someone. To take a human life.'

And that was it. Brooks Matthews launched into his subject without preamble or anecdote. The arguments for and against capital punishment were enumerated evenly. Typical cases were cited briefly. Statistical data was presented—how public opinion changed, whether the death penalty had any effect on the level of violent crime, whether convicts viewed it as a deterrent or not, and what the laws and figures were like in other countries.

Matthews began by standing back a step and solemnly enunciating the facts in his deep, rich voice. Then, gradually, he leaned forward more and more. He pressed his points vigorously, even angrily at times, defending the rights of victims, their families and friends.

'A year, sometimes two years after the event, when the case comes to trial, the victim is just a name, an entry on the ledger at the county morgue. The defendant usually looks harmless and pathetic. The prosecution often isn't allowed to show police photographs of the dead. People don't see the wife with the purple face, her tongue bulging out and the burn-marks on her breasts. They don't see the twelve-year-old boy with stab wounds all over his body and his penis cut off and stuffed in his mouth. The crime has become distant, impersonal, and the victim isn't there to say, "Yes, this, this, this and this were done to me." And the jury doesn't see the survivors, the family and friends whose lives have also been irreparably damaged.'

Now Matthews propped himself on one elbow, facing the audience in a half-turn, emphasizing his remarks with his left hand, which poked the air. Of course our efforts to rehabilitate criminals were token efforts doomed to be ineffectual. Of course the state of our prisons was nightmarish. Of course great strides could be made to reduce the causes of crime. Of course this country needs sensible gun control laws.

But.

Even if we lived in a vastly improved society, people would still kill other people and the question of capital punishment would remain. We should do everything we can to bring about positive change, Matthews believed, but at the same time we should not shrink from our right to exercise the death penalty in certain cases.

'Not just for revenge or punishment or as a deterrent, and not because we think we have a God-given duty to answer a killing with another killing. All of these are part-reasons, and as long as human beings are involved they will be a factor in human decisions. But the overriding point, the simple, unpleasant fact of the matter is—that capital punishment is the only right answer in certain cases. I repeat: in certain cases.'

In conclusion Matthews offered a simple, clear solution: 'I would be glad to see the death penalty consigned for ever to the past, to have it erased permanently from our statute books. If, at the same time, one other change is made in the law. And that is, for all capital offences there will be a mandatory sentence of life in prison *without parole*. If we're prepared to pay that price, it's that simple. But until such time as we have that on the books, I will continue to support the right of the state, of the people, to ask the death penalty in cases where it applies.'

The audience, most of which opposed capital punishment, gave Brooks Matthews a long and loud round of applause. The man came across as honest and fair. He had made his points eloquently, intelligently. Those who were not convinced, who disagreed, nonetheless respected him. Another person making essentially the same argument might have been received coldly, or even with heckles. But not Matthews. He commanded attention and a hearing. For the next twenty minutes he fielded questions from the crowd.

'Sir, you had Judd Taylor killed in the electric chair. He shot and killed a bank guard while committing a robbery. It was an unpremeditated and perhaps even unintentional killing. Why did you feel Taylor should die for that?'

Matthews smiled mirthlessly. 'I still get questions about Judd Taylor, and they're the easiest ones to answer. Of course it was not a premeditated killing, and I'd go so far as to say yes, it probably was unintentional. But Judd Taylor played the game and paid the price. He shouldn't have been carrying that gun—there's a big difference between robbery and armed robbery. In many ways he was exactly the sort of person who should get the death penalty. Without even bothering to think about it, he pulled out a gun and shot someone, an elderly bank guard. And Taylor would do that again in the same situation. But you can't behave that way and expect to get off with a rap on the knuckles, a few years in jail. The Judd Taylors of the world make crime seem casual, they make murder casual. And that's the worst thing that can ever happen to us.'

When it was all over and everyone rose to leave, Jackie felt as if she were coming out of a dream. Matthews had made an impression on her. He was a man of elegance, style and purpose. He was attractive to look at and to listen to, a man of substance. But he had struck a far deeper chord in her. Matthews resembled the man she thought she would never see, the man she could hardly bear to think of, the man she had never known, her lost father, the figure from the dead dreams of the past.

TWO

♦

Jackie thought they would be the first people to arrive at the reception but when they reached Mory's, they found a fair number already in attendance. 'I thought this was going to be a small quiet party,' she said, glancing around the room. 'Looks like we were lucky to get a table.'

'Half of the law school will be here,' Dan said, speaking up to be heard as the noise level rose in the room.

'Oh, there he is,' Jackie said.

Brooks Matthews had arrived, accompanied by the man who had given the introductory speech. Someone brought them drinks and then, with Matthews taking the lead, they began to work their way through the crowd, stopping at every table or cluster of people, shaking hands and exchanging a few words before moving on.

'He looks like he's campaigning for an election already,' Sandy said, and Dan nodded approvingly.

'It won't do him any harm.'

Jackie could hardly take her eyes off Brooks Matthews. He was much closer now and she could see that her first impression had been correct: he really was a good-looking man, a person whose mere presence communicated depth and strength of character as well as the ability to enjoy life fully. Coming into this room full of strangers he did genuinely stand out. Matthews somehow made everyone else look only ordinary.

A few minutes later he turned to their table. They stood and introduced themselves to him. When it was Jackie's turn, she barely managed to get her name out. Matthews smiled and gave her hand a warm, firm squeeze.

'Good to see you here,' he said. 'Thanks for coming along.'

'We enjoyed your talk very much,' Dan said.

'Very much,' Stuart echoed.

'Glad to hear it. Thank you.'

After a few more pleasantries, Matthews promptly moved on to meet another group of people. Jackie tried hard to concentrate on her friends' conversation after that but found it difficult to do so. Her mind was wandering and she kept looking around the room, tracking Brooks Matthews. You're being silly, she told herself. A handshake and a smile knock you over. And his eyes—the way they fixed on you for two or three seconds. A short time, for sure, but time enough to make you feel that you're the only person in the room, that you have his complete attention.

But there was more to it than the physical element. Here was a man who worked in the public arena, who dealt with horrible crimes and punishment, politics and compromise, and yet he seemed to maintain his own strong beliefs and a sense of purpose uncorrupted by everything around him. Oh stop it, Jackie chided herself. You know virtually nothing about him, you're making up all this in your mind. Just forget it.

But there was no doubting the instinctive response Brooks Matthews aroused in her.

'Are you all right?' Sandy asked.

'Just the heat and smoke getting to me,' Jackie said. 'I think I'll go to the ladies' for a minute.'

'Want me to come with you?' Sandy started to rise from her chair.

'No, no, really, I'm okay. I'll be right back.'

Jackie made her way through the crowd and out of the room. She felt better after she had splashed some cold water on her face and she sat bowed over, breathing deeply. She hoped her friends would decide to leave soon. She didn't want to be the one to suggest it, but she had had enough drinking and the party held no further interest for her.

As Jackie came out of the ladies' room, Brooks Matthews was walking along the corridor in her direction.

'We meet again,' he said.

'Hello.'

'I guess you didn't like my talk earlier this evening.'

'Oh, I did,' Jackie said, startled. 'Why?'

'You had no comment to make when I stopped at your table a few minutes ago.'

Does he really remember me, precisely me, out of that crowd, Jackie wondered. But she could tell immediately by the look in his eyes that he did.

'Well I did—enjoy your lecture. Very much so.'

'Good.' Matthews nodded, evidently waiting for more, while Jackie was having trouble putting words together.

'It gave me a lot to think about,' she said finally.

'You mean capital punishment.'

'No, well yes, but not just that.'

'Really? What else?'

Matthews seemed honestly interested and everything suddenly became easier as Jackie realized she was beginning to relax. It was that ability of his to make another person feel important and to know that he wasn't just listening politely to what they had to say.

'Well, it's made me think again about what I'd like to do,' Jackie said. 'Maybe take up law.'

'We need more good women lawyers and judges,' Matthews said. 'What are you studying now?'

'History.'

'That's good background. Are you here at Yale?'

'No, Connecticut College.'

'New London, I know it. Good school. Your name is Jackie, isn't it?'

'That's right.' Good memory, all right, she thought.

'Named after Jacqueline Kennedy, I'll bet.' Matthews smiled broadly. 'Am I right?'

'Yes, how did you know?'

'You look like you were born around nineteen sixty or 'sixty-one and it was a popular name then.'

'Among Democrats,' Jackie added, smiling herself for the first time.

'True enough.' Matthews laughed. 'I worked for Jack in Utah that campaign. It was a good time but it must seem like ancient history to you. Everything is different now and old Democrats like me are drifting to the other side.'

'Someone said you might run for office. Is that true?'

Matthews laughed again. 'Maybe, one of these days. Who knows?' He then nodded his head back towards the reception room. 'Is your boy-friend at Yale?'

'Yes. My date, not boy-friend.'

'I see. Are you around tomorrow at all?' It came out of nowhere, delivered in a smooth, casual manner.

'Uh, I'll be with my friends, but . . .' Jackie didn't know what to say. He wants to see me again?

'Would you care to have breakfast with me? It would be nice to talk some more and this place isn't the best for conversation.'

'I could get up early for coffee,' Jackie said tentatively.

'Good, I'd enjoy that,' Matthews responded enthusiastically. 'The coffee shop of the Park Plaza Hotel at seven-thirty?'

'Yes, all right.'

'You know where it is?'

'Yes.'

'Good, I'll look forward to it. I wouldn't give these lectures and attend the parties if I didn't enjoy them, but it is a tiring circuit and what I really like is the chance to sit down and talk with people in less enforced circumstances . . . you know what I mean?'

'Yes, I think so.'

'Well, I'd better let you get back to your friends now. See you in the morning.'

'Yes, fine,' Jackie said.

Matthews continued in the direction he had been walking and was soon caught up in another conversation. Jackie walked slowly back to the crowded reception-room, slightly confused by what had just transpired. It had all happened so quickly, and yet Matthews made it seem the most natural thing in the world. Had he planned it all, or was it just as innocent as it appeared?

They stayed at the party for another hour, drinking and talking. Something had been released in Jackie and she could sit back, relax and be pleasant company. She even found herself enjoying the Yale stories Dan and Stuart told. Jackie didn't give Brooks Matthews another thought, nor did she once look around the room again to spot him. She didn't have to now.

Poor Stuart, Jackie couldn't help thinking with a smile as she took off her shoes. He is kind of sweet and he means well. Polite. Considerate. Unaggressive. A good, safe, uncomplicated date, and he wasn't unattractive either.

But . . . she had met Brooks Matthews.

Jackie made up the sofa-bed and changed into her nightgown. Then she decided she would have a last drink after all by herself. She poured a small whisky from the bottle Dan and Stuart had brought, added some ice and a lot of water.

Brooks Matthews. What about him now? What indeed. Why did he want to see her again? Jackie Pierce, lowly undergraduate. Perhaps he just wants to see if he can get anywhere with me, like from the coffee shop up to his hotel room. A man who gives lectures at colleges and universities around the country must have a fair amount of success with enthusiastic and very willing female students. Especially a man as attractive as Brooks Matthews. Is that what he thinks, that I'm just one more body who will count herself lucky for the chance of jumping into his bed?

Jackie sipped her whisky. No, it wasn't the man's style. He didn't have that look in his eyes, that look which men can never completely mask and which conveys essential carnal interest. Or had she been too dazzled to notice? Anyhow, he must have found her attractive enough, otherwise he most likely wouldn't have bothered to stop and talk, or extend the invitation.

What then? Breakfast. Coffee. It couldn't go anywhere after that, a brief, pleasant conversation. Jackie had to go off with her friends and Matthews undoubtedly had things to do. People to see, places to go: a man like that doesn't sit around with time to kill. He's probably on a carefully worked out schedule. So, nothing can happen, Jackie told herself.

The simplest explanation was the one which Matthews himself had offered. Maybe he really did like meeting people and chatting informally with them. Besides, a man who is thinking of entering politics is not, if he has any sense, going to risk getting in trouble with a girl, but he might well enjoy having breakfast with one. Any law student, Dan or Stuart for instance, would be delighted to accept such an invitation, so she should simply take advantage of the opportunity and forget about anything else.

But she couldn't. Not entirely.

Because the other side of the coin was the fact that Jackie was undeniably attracted to Brooks Matthews. She couldn't quite acknowledge it to herself, it was such an impossible notion that could never lead anywhere. They lived in completely different worlds, on opposite sides of the country. It was silly to even think about.

THREE

♦

Jackie woke up early that morning, before her alarm was due to go off. The apartment the boys had borrowed for them was chilly and the grey light made it seem stranger and even more unfamiliar. But then, the events of the preceding evening were completely unreal to her now.

As she got up to wash and dress, Jackie noticed that the other bed was undisturbed and empty. So Sandy had decided to spend the night with Dan. Jackie wasn't surprised but in spite of herself she was a little annoyed. She didn't like waking up alone in another city and in the apartment of someone she had never even met. Admit you're a trifle envious too, Jackie argued mentally. Not of Dan in particular, but simply of the fact that Sandy had someone to be with. Jackie turned on the radio for company.

She took a long hot shower, finished off with a quick blast of cold water, and briskly towelled herself dry. Her skin tingled and she felt much better. The sun was higher now, brightening the apartment, and the sounds of the city stirring outside mingled with the voices and music on the radio.

Should she tell her friends that she had been to breakfast with Brooks Matthews, Jackie wondered as she walked down the street. There was no reason to hide the fact, but the more she thought about it the more Jackie became convinced that there was no need to mention it either. She would tell Sandy, of course, but that could wait until they were on their way back to New London tomorrow night.

The coffee shop of the Park Plaza Hotel was large and fairly crowded but Jackie spotted Brooks Matthews almost at once. She was about eight minutes late: just right, she thought. Matthews stood and smiled broadly as she approached his table.

'Good morning,' he greeted her. 'I'm glad you came along. I was afraid you might change your mind.'

'Oh, why?' Jackie sat down opposite him.

'No reason.' Matthews shrugged, still smiling. 'Anyway, you're here now, let's organize some food first.'

'Did you enjoy the party last night?' he asked when the waitress departed.

'Yes, I did. How about you? It was your party.'

'Sure, it was fun, but you're wrong about it being my party. I've been to quite a few of them and they're really for the enjoyment of the law faculty. I'm just the excuse they need to justify the liquor bill.'

Jackie laughed. 'Where do you go from here?'

'Boston, this afternoon. I'll be there for most of the next week.'

'A busy schedule,' Jackie said.

'I'm afraid so. Fortunately, I've got some old friends there, so I won't have to stay in another hotel.'

The food arrived then and for a few moments they ate silently. Jackie had to make an effort not to stare dumbly at the man across the table from her. This close, and in the light of day, Matthews was splendid-looking, and his eyes were the most brilliant, piercing blue Jackie had ever seen.

'Well, tell me about yourself, Jackie. Where are you from originally?'

'Philadelphia.'

Matthews nodded. 'Family there still?'

'Just my aunt,' Jackie said quietly. 'She raised me after my parents died in a car crash when I was small.' Matthews didn't speak, but let his face show sympathy. 'She's a wonderful woman, my aunt,' Jackie added.

'That's something to be grateful for,' Matthews said. 'It would have been even harder on you if you hadn't had someone close to take care of you then.'

'I know. Aunt Josie's been terrific.'

Matthews poured more coffee.

'And now you're studying history. To do what—teach?'

'That's about all you can do with history,' Jackie said with a smile. 'But you got me interested in law last night. I might give that some serious thought.'

'Good.'

'I never really considered it before because it takes a long time and a lot of money to go through law school, doesn't it?'

'It's a long course and hard work,' Matthews agreed. 'But then so are most things worth doing. The important thing is to know what you want and to be sure of it. Then the hard work isn't really work, and you don't notice the time.'

'Yes, well, that's exactly what I'm not sure about, at least not yet,' Jackie said.

'You still have plenty of time to look around and weigh things up before deciding.'

'It must be very difficult for a woman to try to have a career and raise a family at the same time,' Jackie said.

'Yes, but more and more women are doing just that, and there's no reason why they shouldn't if they have the necessary strength of character and discipline.' Matthews toyed with his coffee spoon idly. 'Is that what you hope to do?'

'I think that would be a kind of ideal situation, but I

don't know whether I could handle it.'

'I bet you could,' Matthews said confidently. 'I bet you could do anything you wanted if you set your mind to it.' Again the big smile lit his face.

It suddenly occurred to Jackie that she and Matthews, two complete strangers, were discussing her personal life as if they were old friends. It wasn't what she had expected and Jackie thought there was something vaguely wrong about it. But at the same time it seemed perfectly natural. Besides, sometimes it was much easier to talk about one's personal life with a stranger.

'Are you interested in politics at all?' he asked.

'You *are* running,' Jackie said with a grin.

Matthews smiled sheepishly. 'That was a serious question, young lady. Besides, you don't have a vote in Utah.'

'True enough. I guess you could say I'm interested in politics to the extent that I get a little depressed every time I see the President on television and think, God, he's supposed to be leading our country.'

'I know how you feel,' Matthews said.

'It seems like everything's in a mess and nobody is really trying to do anything about it.'

'There are some good people in politics,' Matthews allowed, 'but not enough of them. Some of those old boys in Washington have this country sewed up.'

'You should run,' Jackie declared impulsively, her enthusiasm suddenly growing. 'You have strong ideas and would fight for them.'

Matthews nodded indulgently. 'I may just do that. I've been practising law for twenty years now, more or less, and I'm beginning to feel like a change would do me good.'

'What does your wife think?' Jackie astounded herself with the question, which just popped out apparently of its own volition. But before she had time to feel foolish Matthews surprised her with his reply.

'Oh, I haven't been married in years. That was long ago. My first wife, she truly was a fine woman and we were very happy together. But—' Matthews's features tightened—'she developed bone cancer and there was nothing they could do about it.'

'Oh God,' Jackie whispered.

'She died when she was twenty-five. It was one of those terrible tragedies life sometimes inflicts on people. And then I went and did something really dumb, I got married again. Looking back, it's easy to see I was trying to start a new life and erase the pain, but it was too fast and just plain wrong. We got divorced after about a year or so and I learned an expensive lesson. Since then I've been married to my work, I guess you could say.' Matthews looked as if he had more to say but he remained silent.

'I'm sorry. I didn't know.' Jackie still couldn't understand why she had asked the question in the first place. Until that moment she hadn't thought at all about whether or not Matthews was married. Perhaps she had subconsciously assumed that he had a wife . . .

'Nothing to be sorry about,' Matthews declared cheerfully. 'That was a long time ago. Want some more coffee?'

'No, thanks, I'm fine,' Jackie said.

'You have to go and meet your friends at some point, don't you?'

Jackie glanced at her watch. 'In a while,' she said, making it sound like she was in no hurry at all. She was enjoying Matthew's company and would have been happy to sit and chat with him all morning.

'Got time for a stroll around the Green?'

'Sure.' Jackie was delighted.

'Good.'

Matthews paid the bill and they walked slowly out on to the street.

'I love autumn,' he said. 'Some people don't but I do. The leaves may be falling but how can you walk in this lovely sharp air and not feel really alive?'

'You're right, it is beautiful out. Even in the city.'

'Especially in the city,' Matthews asserted without elaboration. 'And if you shiver a little at least you know your system is working, right?'

Unhurried, they made their way across the Green, New Haven's downtown park, admiring the stately elm trees and old churches which graced the scene. The leaf-strewn grass crunched underfoot in patches where the night's frost still lingered.

'What was the Judd Taylor case all about?' Jackie asked. 'I'm sorry to be ignorant, but—'

'Not at all,' Matthews interrupted. 'It happened back before you were born, so there's no reason why you should know about it. It wasn't much of anything anyhow, though it did me a lot of good at the time. The newspapers made a big deal out of it, and out of Judd Taylor,' he said with a grimace. 'But the fact is, Judd Taylor was nothing more than a small-time crook. He also happened to be loudmouthed and arrogant, which always impresses some people and that's why he developed a following of sorts. You know, there are some people who have nothing better to do than become cops 'n' robbers fans, and they follow crime like it was the stock market. To them Judd Taylor was entertainment, the guy who stayed one step ahead of the police, and they liked it that way.'

'Where did this all take place?' Jackie asked.

'Utah mostly, that's my home territory. Taylor was a bank robber and he made a few raids into Colorado and Arizona, but we caught him in Utah and that's where the trial was held.'

'Well, what was so special about a bank robber? I mean, why would that case cause so much—'

'He killed a bank guard, as was bound to happen sooner or later, so it was a murder trial. And when it was all over Taylor got the electric chair.'

'I see,' Jackie said.

'The reason it did me good was that it was my first big case. It was a little tricky, at least to someone fresh from law school, and I won it. That's what people remember. I've prosecuted dozens, oh, maybe a hundred more important cases since then, but you won't hear about them. People love a sensation and that's all Judd Taylor was, a local sensation for a little while. Kind of silly, isn't it?'

'How old was he?'

'Taylor—oh, he was in his early twenties at the time. Twenty-two, twenty-three, I don't recall exactly.'

They walked along without speaking for a few minutes, just enjoying the air, the sunshine and each other's presence.

'You know, it's a funny thing,' Matthews said at last, 'but I really like being with young people, someone like yourself, a lot more than the boring old legal types I have to deal with most of the time. That's one of the reasons I've been thinking about entering politics. I'd like to build a team of bright young people who have ideas and energy, and still have the belief that it is possible to accomplish something worthwhile these days.'

'That's good,' Jackie said.

'The more you see of this world, the harder it is to maintain the hopes and expectations you start out with when you're young. Most people lose them over the years, they come to accept things the way they are—and they call that being adult or realistic. Well, damn it all, I'm not like that. I could keep on doing what I'm doing, making a handsome living at the law profession.' Matthews stopped and turned to Jackie. 'But that would be easy, and I know I can do more. Too many people are in politics for what they can get, but nobody owns me.'

'I hope you make it,' Jackie said sincerely. 'A lot of people would like to be able to believe in government again.'

'That's right. And sometimes you've got to try something even if you aren't sure whether it'll work or not.' Matthews looked suddenly intense, completely caught up in what he was saying. 'Do you know what I'm talking about?'

'Yes I do, and I think you're right.' Jackie didn't understand why Brooks Matthews was telling her all this but she found it oddly moving. Here was a man in his late forties who was ready to change his life dramatically because he believed it was the right thing to do.

'I'm not afraid of taking risks,' Matthews said.

Jackie was about to make some remark but then it dawned on her that Matthews might be talking about more than going into politics. His eyes held hers and the searching expression on his face seemed to charge the air with unspoken possibilities.

'Neither am I,' Jackie said directly, her voice now firm and certain.

'I know. I can see it in you.'

They resumed walking. But the silence between them was shared now. Something had passed between them in that brief moment, a feeling of real contact. Jackie Pierce and Brooks Matthews were no longer quite strangers to each other.

To Jackie, it was a wonderfully warm feeling, an unexpected joy born of a chance and seemingly casual encounter. She knew that she would soon go to meet her friends again and that Matthews would leave for Boston, but that didn't make her sad. Now is the right time to say goodbye, she thought. Now, with as few words as possible to diminish what had transpired. Now, before the spell was broken from within by some foolish remark or act.

And it happened the right way.

They found themselves back on the west side of the Green, opposite the Park Plaza Hotel. Matthews held Jackie's hand tightly in both of his. They said goodbye and parted.

FOUR

♦

When the bell rang signalling the end of the school day, Sally Yates did not join her friends who were going to Ken's Kampus, a nearby coffee shop. She had already told them she had an errand to do today, so while several hundred students poured out of the high school, Sally sat waiting in a cubicle in the girls' lavatory.

Five minutes. Ten minutes. A bit longer, then the building was quiet and Sally felt reasonably sure that all of her friends were gone; only students on detention and the teachers remained behind.

Sally examined herself in the washroom mirror. Seventeen and blonde, a pretty face, attractive hair. Sally liked to think that she looked a little like Cheryl Ladd. She worked hard to maintain a healthy, well-scrubbed appearance. She had a good figure and if at times she worried about being a trifle tall, today she knew that would be no problem. He was decidedly taller.

Sally applied fresh lip gloss, gathered her things and left the school in a hurry. She didn't want to be a minute late. What if he doesn't wait? What if he doesn't even turn up at all? Perhaps he would see Sally's friends, assume that she was absent from school today for some reason, and leave. No, he had to be there. He hadn't missed a day in more than a week, hanging around the same corner, smiling, giving Sally the eye. She had always been walking with her friends and had hardly bothered to acknowledge the young man's existence. But today would be different.

She wore her best plaid skirt and an elegant white blouse, with a Liberty silk scarf tied fashionably around her neck. Although it was a bracing autumn day, she left her coat open.

He wasn't in high school, Sally was sure of that. Which was a good thing as far as she was concerned. She had a steady date, Mark Paulsen, and she was supposed to see him this evening when he finished work at the supermarket. Mark was in Sally's class at school, he was handsome enough, got good grades and worked hard at his part-time job. And at school you had to be going with someone. But, for all of that, Mark was still only a student. He was lacking in something, Sally wasn't sure what. Not adventurous enough, or exciting. Perhaps it was just that she had set her sights higher and knew that theirs was nothing more than a high school romance, bound to run its course and end around graduation. Mark would probably be happy in Utah for the rest of his life. But Sally was planning to be in Los Angeles a year from now.

The young man on the street corner, however, was not at all like Mark. One look told Sally that. He was in his early twenties, she reckoned, and looked like he'd been around. Maybe he had been in the army. Definitely not a college boy (what would he be doing in a town like this?), and definitely not someone to get seriously involved with (no one was). But still, he could prove to be enjoyable in the short-term. Los Angeles was a year away and Sally was beginning to think that her life could do with livening up.

And there he was.

As she turned the corner on to King Street she could see the young man lounging on the corner a block away. Sally forced herself to slow down, changing her stride. Today her eyes would be on him all the way as she approached and passed. She would almost smile at him, but not quite, and she would try to match the knowing look in his eyes. Then it would be up to him.

As on the previous days, he wore faded jeans, scuffed cowboy boots, a bright shirt and a rawhide jacket. He was tall and thin but he looked solid; rangy, Sally thought. He was not wildly handsome she noticed, now that she looked at him carefully, but there was something completely engaging about his expression, the contrast between that boyishly charming smile and those hungry, adult eyes.

The pattern, already established, repeated itself and he let her pass. Oh hell, Sally thought, he's not going to do anything. He just hangs around street corners and watches high school girls go by. He's not interested in me at all.

But then he came along from behind and fell into step beside her. Sally tried not to appear startled.

'Hi,' he said.

'Hi.' God, how could one tiny word sound so nervous?

'Mind if I walk with you a little?'

Sally shrugged as if to say that it was a free country and he could do whatever he liked.

'Where you goin'?'

'Home,' she answered.

'Where's that?'

'I don't know you,' Sally said. Let him work.

'I didn't mean to seem nosey. It's just that I'm new to this town and I don't know anybody yet. And I was wondering if you felt like taking a walk through the park . . .'

'It's not exactly on my way,' Sally said.

'Ah come on, it's such a nice afternoon and there aren't many left before winter sets in. You could maybe tell me a bit about this town of yours I've landed in.'

'Okay,' Sally laughed.

'Good,' the young man said happily. 'Here, let me carry those books for you.'

'I can tell you all you need to know about this town in ten seconds,' Sally said as they cut across the street to the park.

'Really?'

'It's dull and boring, there's nothing to do and so nothing happens. It's small, and small-minded.'

The young man chuckled. 'Everybody loves to hate their own hometown. But to me this place looks kinda nice.'

'It's a good place to come on a honeymoon if you've only got two days,' Sally said. 'They'll seem longer here.'

The young man laughed obligingly. 'That's the official town joke, I bet. Well, maybe this place is on the quiet side, but every now and again you find yourself ready to enjoy that. Cities can get to be a pain and then you need to get away from them to rest a spell.'

'Is that what you're doing here?' Sally asked.

'I guess so. Kinda.'

'What do you do?'

'Not a lot, to tell you the truth,' the young man said, smiling sheepishly. 'I work around at this and that, see what's goin' on. I've been to a lot of places, work a bit, get bored, move along to the next place. Never found anywhere I liked enough to want to stay.'

'Well there's nothing much happening here,' Sally said. 'But you might enjoy it for a while.' Time to warm up a little, she thought. This could be all right. A good-looking guy just passing through town. She could imagine how her girl-friends would react: they'd be knocked out. Mark would be temporarily demoted to number two, the high school date.

They walked slowly through the park, taking the long way around. The young man spoke for a while, telling Sally of towns and cities he'd been through, jobs he'd worked, funny incidents and occasional troubles. Sally listened attentively. Maybe he wasn't the most intelligent or sophisticated man in the world, but he was sharp in his own way and he obviously knew how to take care of himself. He didn't talk about women, but Sally was sure he'd known more than a few. A woman can tell that in a man, she thought. Maybe it was because he didn't have to try to be sexy, he just was. But Sally didn't notice that for all his talk the young man actually said very little of any substance about himself.

They sat on a bench and smoked a couple of cigarettes, talking quietly. His words had soon taken on a kind of magic of their own and Sally was drifting along on the sound of his voice. It was strong, sometimes even hard, but always reassuring. Like her father's had been when she was a child.

When he suddenly said 'Tell me about you,' Sally opened up immediately, explaining to the young man how school was boring, how the town was boring, how her friends and family were nice but unexciting and how she planned to go to Los Angeles to college in a year's time. College would probably be boring too, but what she really wanted was to be in Los Angeles. If, after the first year, she was fed up with college, she would get a job. Even if she had to start as a secretary, she was sure she could work her way into a really good position. Advertising, music, films, the media—who knows? The possibilities were almost endless.

The young man agreed. He had been to Los Angeles once and he could see the attraction, even if it didn't particularly suit him. She was a bright, attractive young woman and she had nothing to lose and everything to gain by getting out there and seeing what the world was all about. Plenty of people went to LA with foolish dreams, he told her, dreams that would come to nothing.

'But it's a sin to have no dreams at all, and if you don't try you'll never know.'

'That's right,' Sally said. 'If you don't take the chance you'll always wonder what you might have achieved.'

'Exactly.'

Sally found it very easy to be with this young man. It's not at all like being with Mark or a girl-friend, she thought. You could talk to a stranger about things you would find it impossible to mention with someone you knew. If she ever told Mark what Los Angeles meant to her, he would smile that indulging smile of his and then tell her to get her feet back on the ground and not be silly.

This guy was a find, and Sally congratulated herself on the way she had handled the situation so far. They rose to leave the park in the gathering dusk.

'I live on Hillside Crescent. In that direction,' Sally said, pointing.

'I went by there the other day,' the young man said. 'I know where it is. We can go this way.'

'Right.' Was he following me home 'the other day', Sally wondered? If so, great. She had decided to do her best to keep this fellow in town indefinitely. She liked him and he obviously was interested in her, so . . .

They had come around to the topside of the park and now he was steering Sally to High Rock, a secluded little clearing that overlooked the centre of town. She knew this at once and she didn't mind because she had it all worked out in advance. There would be some heavy kissing and a preview of more —just enough to make sure he came back. Preferably tomorrow. But if he really pushed it, she could make excuses to Mark tonight.

'This is really pretty,' he said as they came along the narrow path. 'You get a really pretty view of the town.'

'You haven't been here before?'

'I only got in town a few days ago, no.'

'It's a popular spot when the weather's warm,' she said, shifting her weight from foot to foot, trying to send a signal without appearing impatient.

'I'm sure it is.'

The young man carefully placed Sally's school books on the ground and turned to her.

'It's getting dark,' she said.

'You know what?'

'What?'

'You're just the girl I've been looking for.' That silky firm voice filling the air irresistibly.

Sally didn't say anything. She looked at him. He's taking his time but it's nice, she thought. He took her face in his hands and kissed her gently, lovingly. Sally wasn't really thinking but she noticed he wasn't a fast groper like the boys at school. Yes, this man knew women. One arm around her shoulder, the other hand to the small of her back, he held her close.

'I like you.' She hadn't meant to say a thing, but the words came out.

He kissed her again, longer and deeper.

'Hey, you know what?' he whispered.

'Hmmmn?'

'You haven't told me your name.'

She smiled. 'Sally. What's yours?'

'Goodbye, Sally,' he said, moving back a step.

The hand came around and the blade whizzed by in a flash. It cut so deep that Sally Yates was nearly decapitated on the spot. The young man jumped back a few paces. Blood spurted obscenely, the girl's eyes fluttered and rolled blindly. A terrible noise came from her throat, a raucous buzzing and popping, and then she toppled backwards to the ground, hands motioning aimlessly.

It didn't take long for her to die, and when she did the young man knelt down over the body.

FIVE

◆

He's crazy, she thought, and I'm even crazier.

In the week following her visit to New Haven, Jackie spent a good deal of time mulling over her meeting with Brooks Matthews. She wanted to make her own personal and private sense of it, and by so doing secure its proper place in her memory and experience.

At first Jackie was inclined to play down the strength of her response to Matthews and the significance of their exchange. She was determined not to paint a rosy, romantic picture in her mind, or in any way to sustain a false idea of what had happened. She would not give herself the benefit of the doubt. Common sense and a little distance told Jackie the next day that her breakfast and walk with Matthews had not been as momentous as she might like to think. In the circumstances, they had had an unusually open and personal conversation, and that was good, but it didn't, couldn't lead to anything more. Nor could Jackie assume that their walk and words had touched Matthews in the same way, to the same degree, that they had her.

And yet . . .

If her response to Matthews was so strong and true, then wasn't that enough? Couldn't she just accept that moment for what it was, for what it meant to her alone, and be pleased it had happened at all?

Yes, but . . .

By Tuesday Jackie was fed up with herself. She broke her mood in a simple act of will, making up her mind that it was foolish to let the Matthews incident become an obsession. Almost at once she felt better.

That night she received a telephone call from Brooks Matthews in Boston.

'I hope you don't mind my calling.'

'No, not at all, of course not,' Jackie said, confused and startled. 'It's nice to hear from you . . . I didn't think I would.'

'You know, I enjoyed Saturday morning with you and so I decided to see if I could get through to you.'

Interesting choice of words, Jackie thought.

'The Registrar's Office gave me your dorm number,' Matthews continued.

It was nearly ten o'clock and the Registrar's Office closed at five that afternoon, so Jackie knew this was no spur-of-the-moment phone call.

'I won't tell you how long it's been since the last time I rang up a college girl at her dormitory. So long it feels brand new to me—but good.'

Jackie giggled.

They stayed on the line together for forty minutes. Matthews did most of the talking: the talks and seminars he was giving in Boston, the latest nonsensical news item from Washington, the Kennedy campaign of 1960 and how much it meant to him, crank letters he occasionally received and how this trip east strengthened his belief that going into politics was the right thing to do.

'When?' Jackie asked.

'Oh, not for a couple of years yet. I've got some unfinished business to look after first, and there are a lot of preparations that have to be made, but I'm working on it now. Just don't tell *Newsweek*.'

'I'm very discreet.'

'Good, good.'

Jackie didn't get to sleep until late that night. She made a large mug of hot chocolate and sat on her bed, knees up under her chin, replaying the phone call in her mind. If Matthews needed someone to talk to, it was pretty clear she was the one. She had been right all along.

He phoned again the next night and they talked for more than an hour. Jackie was entranced. The telephone had become a magic device and the rich, charming voice that reached her ear commanded Jackie's complete attention. She felt that she was beginning to get a real understanding of what kind of man Brooks Matthews was.

After the second phone call Jackie found Sandy making coffee in the second-floor lounge of the dorm.

'I'll have a cup too,' Jackie said. 'Brooks just called again.'

'Aha, he really is keen.'

'I know.'

'How about you?'

'Are you kidding? He's fantastic. That's just the problem.'

'Why?'

'Oh Sandy, you know as well as I do that it can't lead to anything.'

'So what? Take it one day at a time, slow and easy. If you enjoy talking with him, that's fine. Don't expect anything and you won't get hurt.'

'Thanks, that's easy to say.'

'Is he coming on heavy?'

'No, not really,' Jackie admitted. 'But obviously he likes me.'

'So why can't you just regard him as a new acquaintance, a friend?'

'I'm trying.'

'Here, get this inside of you,' Sandy said, passing Jackie a steaming cup of instant coffee.

'Thanks.'

'Besides, isn't he going back to Utah or some damn place like that?'

'Yes.'

'So relax,' Sandy said. 'If he starts phoning you every night from all the way out there, and flying in on weekends, then you'll have something to think about. But not now. Now all you've got is a walk in the park and a couple of phone calls.'

'I know, but—'

'You're afraid it'll be like Todd Jackson all over again, aren't you? That he'll set you up and then let you down. Jackie, you're a year older and a lot wiser.'

'I wish.' Jackie smiled wanly.

'Really,' Sandy insisted. 'Besides, he's a bigshot lawyer out on the other side of the country. It's not the same at all.'

'He asked me to meet him in New York this week-end.'

Sandy's eyebrows arched.

'Oh boy. What did you say?'

'I said yes.'

'Oh boy.'

'Do you think I did the wrong thing?' Jackie asked earnestly.

'No, you're a big girl, you can take care of yourself. But go with both eyes open and don't build up any silly ideas ahead of time. Where are you going to stay?'

'Some hotel. He's going to reserve a separate room for me.'

'Mmmn-hmmn.' Sandy grinned. 'I'll bet you a dollar it has a connecting door.'

He's crazy, she thought as the train approached Manhattan, and I'm even crazier. A week ago he and I had never met, never even known the other existed.

They found each other attractive, very attractive. And she was sure it would be a good week-end, because they enjoyed each other's company, they could talk comfortably together. But he definitely was going back to Utah, and she was going back to college. How would she feel on Monday?

Matthews was waiting for her in the Oyster Bar at Grand Central Station, as planned.

'The Carlyle is a great old hotel,' Matthews said as the cab headed uptown. 'It's not one of those modern monstrosities that makes you feel like you're staying in an airport. And the service is excellent. Jack Kennedy used to stay there.'

'Brooks, I know you want the whole thing to be your treat—'

'Absolutely.'

'But I'm going to pay for my room.'

Matthews cocked his head a little to one side.

'Oh, no, no,' he said.

'Yes, I mean it. Please.'

Her voice was quiet but determined and Matthews knew at once that it was an important point to Jackie.

'All right, if that's what you want.'

'I do.'

A few minutes later they arrived at the Carlyle. Jackie checked in and was taken to her room. After unpacking and changing, she was to meet Matthews in the bar downstairs.

In the meantime he busied himself studying the show listings in the newspaper. Finally he made his choice and bought a couple of tickets at the desk.

That evening they dined at *21* and stayed late, drinking champagne. The conversation was relaxed and freewheeling, never forced. Jackie felt pleasantly high, the effect of having a good time with Matthews and sipping her Moët at the right pace.

'I admire you,' Matthews said at one point. 'I like the way you conduct yourself—does that sound silly?'

'Yes,' Jackie teased.

'Well, I do.' Matthews smiled at himself. 'You're not aggressive, like a lot of women are these days. But you follow your own course. I can see a measure of independence and confidence.'

Jackie didn't know whether to blush and say thanks, or simply to laugh. His observations didn't agree at all with the way she saw herself.

'Do you miss your mother and father?' Matthews asked suddenly. His expression had grown serious, even urgent. Jackie stared at the bubbles in her drink. 'If you don't want to talk about it—' Matthews left the unfinished sentence hanging in the air.

'No, I don't mind,' Jackie said. 'It's hard to say accurately what I feel about them, that's all. I don't remember much—I was only three when they died.'

'Ah.'

'I can picture them in my mind, and I have photographs, of course. I can remember a few happy incidents, but not a great deal. How can you miss two people you never had a chance to get to know? But I do, I do miss them, in a way. They're missing in my life.'

'I know what you mean.'

'It must be harder for you, with your first wife. You knew her, you were in love.'

Matthews hunched his shoulders. 'At least we had each other for a while. But I'll tell you something. It wasn't until long after her death that I saw how selfish my attitude had been during her illness.'

'What do you mean?'

'I used to get really angry with her, not to her face, but I would have these seething black rages because of what she was doing to me. I knew she was dying and I hated her for it. Amazing, isn't it, the way people react.'

'You were in a terrible situation, the sheer helplessness of it—'

'Yes, but she was the one who was dying. Only much later, after that disaster of a second marriage, did I begin to understand it.'

At which point, Jackie thought, you gave yourself entirely to your work.

'Brooks.'

'Yes?' Matthews refilled her glass, then his own.

'Why did you invite me to breakfast last week, when you didn't even know me, and then here to New York?'

For once Matthews shifted his gaze from Jackie to the table. 'At Yale—I don't know, I just did. Does there have to be a reason?'

'Do you do that often, at other colleges?'

'Jackie—'

'I'm sorry, that was unfair. Forget it.'

'No, no, it's all right,' Matthews insisted, his eyes now dominating her again. 'You can always ask me anything you want.' He paused briefly, then continued. 'I meet a lot of people all the time, in my work and when I'm on the lecture circuit. That's inevitable. But only rarely, very rarely, do I meet someone I really like, and like being with, someone I would want to make a friend. I feel that way about you. Okay?'

Jackie nodded, slightly ashamed of herself for having asked the question, or at least for phrasing it the way she did. What, after all, would she say if he asked her why she had accepted his invitations? Nonetheless, she was pleased with his reply.

He squeezed her hand.

'You're slowing down,' he said, raising one finger to point at the champagne.

When they got back to the Carlyle, Jackie discovered that Matthews had the room directly across the corridor from hers, so he said good night to her at her door. He gave her a fatherly kiss on the cheek, and then another, more romantic, but surprisingly gentle one on her lips.

'Be careful, Mr Matthews,' Jackie said, her voice low and husky. 'Someone might see you.'

Whether or not she actually intended that to sound

like an invitation, Matthews merely smiled.

'Sleep well,' he said.

'And you.'

Alone in her room, Jackie felt good. They had had a fine evening and, while she knew she would probably let Matthews in if he came knocking at her door, she appreciated the fact that he wasn't pushing, manoeuvring, trying to get her in bed as quickly as possible. That's maturity, and respect, she thought. He was letting things move at their own natural speed.

Saturday, they spent running around New York like two tourists trying to cram in as much as possible on a brief stopover. They went to the Museum of Modern Art, to Bloomingdale's for a spot of people-watching, to the Fulton Market where they bought and ate raw shrimp in the open air, to Little Italy for mid-afternoon spaghetti and clams, and to the top of the World Trade Center.

After a rest and a change of clothing back at the hotel, they went to P. J. Clarke's for drinks and then on to the theatre to see *Annie*. The seats were not the best, but neither Brooks nor Jackie seemed to mind, so caught up were they in each other's company.

Jackie was giving herself completely to this weekend, regardless of how it might turn out. So far, she thought, her attitude was being proven right. If she never saw Brooks again she would still have this memory and, more important, the knowledge that her reaction to their walk around the Green in New Haven a week ago had been true. For both of them.

After the show, they had steaks and drinks at an unlikely-looking but excellent place called Charlie's. Matthews was in an expansive, jovial mood.

'A friend of mine from Rutgers first took me here,' he said. 'We knocked back bourbons until I lost. This place is so close to Eighth Avenue it has no right to be good, but it is.'

'That's New York.'

After eating they stayed for a couple of nightcaps.

The Saturday-night crowd was colourful and noisy. Watching them, and the man she was with, Jackie felt as if she were in an endless, timeless moment, a spectacle that lived and grew on itself, for itself. A rare moment when, for no particular reason, life finally seems to be what it always should be. Joy. Her other life, in Philadelphia, at college, seemed so distant and different as to belong to another person altogether. Flat, two-dimensional, a world composed in shades of grey. I'm out of that and far away, Jackie thought dreamily. I don't know where yet, but it feels good, it feels right.

'What a marvellous day,' she said aloud.

Matthews nodded in agreement. 'And I was worried.' He chuckled at himself.

'Were you? Why?'

'Oh, I didn't think you would even want to come and see me here in New York. And then when you said yes, I began to think—it's not going to go well, she's going to have a lousy time. That sort of thing.'

'Why? That's—'

'Hell, I'm close to thirty years older than you. That's why. You might find me a silly old bore, you know. I've never been to a disco in my life.'

Jackie laughed warmly.

'Good, because I don't like discos,' she said. 'And I've been having a wonderful time. You're not boring, old or silly.'

'Good. I haven't enjoyed myself so much in a long, long time.'

'Same here. And by the way,' Jackie added. 'We're even.'

'Hmmn?'

'I was worried too.'

'Really? About what?'

'That I'm nearly thirty years younger than you, that I'd strike you as just a silly child, a student, not brilliant or witty or charming. I mean, you must meet a lot of women—'

'Who think they're so smart and witty and charming,' Matthews cut in. 'Yes, and they try so hard to maintain their image of who they should be, to keep their repartee sharp, their sex lives exotic, their politics in fashion and their fashions so "natural". Yes, you're right, I have met a lot of women.' Matthews's voice had lowered but his tone was more urgent. 'Don't become one of them, Jackie.'

'Women you've had affairs with?'

Matthews sat back, smiling. 'You would make a good lawyer,' he said. 'You come up with some punchy questions. The answer is, no, that's not what I meant. Don't become that kind of woman. Who tries to be something.'

'I know what you meant.'

'Good. The rest is quite straightforward. I don't fool around and in twenty years I've only had two or three—encounters—that looked as if they might grow into something, but didn't. It may sound like I'm bragging, but I'm not, it's the miserable truth: a lot of women push themselves my way for one reason or another, and nothing turns me off more.'

In the taxi, returning to the hotel, Jackie let her head rest on Matthews's shoulder. Nothing was said between them but it seemed natural and right. He put his arm around her, not unlike a father holding a tired child at the end of an exhausting day of fun.

The spell continued as Matthews opened the door and took Jackie into his room. As he removed her coat their eyes locked and he was moved by the searching but hopeful expression she wore. Her features seemed to be saying, here I am, don't be unkind to me.

Jackie's own thoughts were in turmoil. She was about to cross a line, she knew, an important psychological boundary. But now it was what she wanted, and she sensed the same in Brooks. They had to discover the truth about each other, regardless of the emotional risk. They had talked together intensely during the past week and it all led up to this moment of final intimacy.

Brooks Matthews became Jackie's lover that night. He kissed her long and passionately. They were both a little nervous, trembling in each other's embrace, but that too was good and as it should be for two people who seemed to be discovering an eternal pleasure for the first time.

Jackie was passive, caught up in an enormous wave of feeling, surrendering completely, lying back but responding to his every move, his lightest touch. Brooks made love to her slowly, tenderly, leading all the way but allowing each delicious moment find itself and absorb them in the whole great rhythm of the act.

Later, much later, when Jackie finally began to drift off to sleep, she felt like a new person who had arrived in a wondrous new land. Dreams and reality became one.

They slept in each other's arms. She was happier and more at peace than she had ever been in her life.

SIX

♦

Early in the morning they made love again. The room was semi-dark, the sex lazy and beautiful. Two people still mostly asleep, communing perfectly in body and dream. Jackie felt like a cloud, floating serenely high above the rest of the world. She could stay this way for ever.

At some point she woke up, perhaps because Brooks was no longer beside her in bed. Jackie turned her head slightly and saw that he was sitting in one of the armchairs across the room. He had on a dark blue robe and he seemed lost in thought, so much so that he didn't notice when she sat up looking at him.

'Brooks,' she said softly.

He turned to her and his face immediately lit up with a glowing smile. Her hair was mussed but lovely, reaching almost to her perfectly formed breasts, and he thought she looked so beautiful he couldn't find words. Matthews came over and sat beside her. Jackie opened his robe a little and put the side of her face to his chest. They sat clinging to each other that way for several long minutes.

'I can hear your heart,' Jackie said.

'Can you?'

'Mmmn-hmmn.'

'What does it say?'

'Mmmmmmmn.'

'What's that mean?' Matthews asked, kissing the top of her head.

'I don't know, but it sounds good.'

'Shall I tell you?'

'Yes please,' little girl-ish, looking up at him.

Matthews took her by the shoulders and made her sit back against the pillows to face him. He looked so serious that Jackie was suddenly alert and fearful. This is goodbye coming, she thought. Inevitable, but why first thing in the morning?

'Jackie, I want to marry you.'

Her mouth opened slightly in amazement. That little sentence blindsided her, unleashing a torrent of confused and conflicting emotions.

'I'm serious,' Matthews continued. 'I've given it a lot of thought and I know I'm right. Will you marry me?'

'Brooks—' she managed finally, but then hesitated, still stunned and incapable of putting her thoughts into words.

'I love you, Jackie.' His voice seemed incredibly strong and certain.

'Brooks—I have to think.'

'Of course, of course. We can talk whenever you're ready. I'll order up some coffee and food in the meantime.'

'I don't want anything.'

Jackie got out of bed, grabbed her overcoat and wrapped it around her naked body, and then shut herself in the bathroom. She sat down on the floor, putting her back against the door.

Matthews phoned room service and requested breakfast for two, hoping that Jackie might want some after all. It seemed an odd thing to be doing while his marriage proposal was undergoing active consideration, but he reasoned that the sheer normalcy of breakfast might help in some small way. After he had given his order and hung up the phone, Matthews stretched out on the bed, shutting his eyes but not allowing himself to doze.

A large number of reasons for saying no paraded through Jackie's mind. He was too old. She was too young. They had only met a week ago. Aunt Josie would drop dead. She was at college, studying for a degree. He lives so far away. He's just infatuated, and so was she for that matter. It wouldn't last. Couldn't. It was impossible, the whole thing was crazy, any way you looked at it. Remember Todd Jackson, she told herself, remember, remember. Jumping into a steady relationship would be risky enough, but marriage . . .

And yet, she wanted more than anything to say yes, to run away with Brooks, to be his lover and wife, and thus to transform her life in an instant. Her heart cried yes, it's right, it's true, don't throw it away, even as her mind argued no, there are too many problems.

Matthews approached the bathroom door.

'Are you crying, Jackie?'

'Yes,' the voice sounding miserable.

'Oh honey, why?'

'I don't know.'

He started to say something but then restrained himself. She had to work this out alone; then they could talk.

The telephone rang, startling both of them. Matthews hurried to answer it.

'Brooks, it's Larry. Sorry to bother you but I figured you'd want to hear the news and I didn't think it would get in the New York Sundays.'

'Okay, what is it?'

'Our friend's got another one.'

'The Blade?'

'Yep, he got a high school girl. Less'n twenty miles from here.'

'God damn. When did this happen?'

'Friday. I tried to get you yesterday, but—'

'Was she still alive when they found her? Did she have a chance to say anything?' Matthews's features were tensed and his mind was transported hundreds of miles away from New York by this sudden interruption.

'No way, Brooks. You know how that sonuvabitch operates. Damn near cut her head clean off.'

'Any leads? Anything at all to go on?'

'Not much, I'm afraid. A couple of her high school friends told us about a young guy who's been hanging around the school every day for the last week or so, and nobody knew him. But if he was the killer, he's sure to be long gone now.'

Matthews bit his lower lip. 'Did they give you a good description?'

'You know what kids are like,' Larry said. 'He looks kinda cute, or he looks different, and so on. We've pieced something together but I'd be surprised if anything came of it.'

'Okay, Larry, you know the routine.'

'We're on it.'

'I'll see you in a day or two.'

'Right.'

Matthews replaced the receiver and sat on the edge of the bed, staring grimly at the floor. He didn't need this, not now. His unfinished business back in Utah, a bloody murderer nicknamed The Blade rearing his ugly head again. This made five victims in less than a year, five young girls savagely killed and mutilated. One sick man was terrorizing the entire state. The police were under heavy pressure from all sides to break it and bring The Blade to justice, and Matthews was intimately involved with the case, following every step of the investigation. Not because he really wanted to be, but because it was a foregone conclusion that when the police finally caught the killer, Matthews would be the man to prosecute him in court. There was no way out of it: even the Governor had spoken to him about it. Matthews didn't relish the prospect because he knew that entering politics immediately after conducting a big, sensational trial, would strike some people as mere opportunism. Well, he would just have to overcome that charge when the time came. Maybe The Blade would commit suicide, as a fair number of murderers do, revolted by their crimes, or perhaps he would be killed when the police tracked him down. Either would be a convenient end to Brooks's inconvenient unfinished business.

In the bathroom, Jackie had heard most of Brooks's side of the conversation and it had a curious effect on her. Without knowing what it was all about she understood that Brooks was involved in something serious and important. Someone had been killed. Her own concerns seemed smaller now. Jackie had been enjoying herself immensely, riding a fantastic high, but suddenly another side of the real world had appeared and she began to see what her role might be.

Brooks loved her and needed her, and those were the two most important things in a relationship. She loved Brooks, but did she really need him? How could she let him go, how could she return to the humdrum life of a lowly undergraduate? Brooks was a rare find and she knew how unlikely it was that she would ever meet another man who had so much to offer. He was distinguished in his field, highly successful, a man going places. And he felt very strongly about her. If she passed him up now, Jackie knew she would regret it for the rest of her life. She would be haunted by what might have been, always wondering, never knowing.

But have no illusions, she told herself. It may just be a bubble, ready to burst at any moment. Stay with it, yes, ride with it, see what it is really made of, but be prepared for anything. You're a big girl now, you can look after yourself, like Sandy said.

Jackie unlocked the bathroom door and came back into the bedroom.

'Hi,' she said meekly, a nervous smile flickering briefly around her mouth.

Brooks brightened and stood up. 'Are you all right?' he asked with evident concern.

'Yes,' Jackie nodded. 'I'm all right.'

For a moment they stood apart there, looking at each other across the room. Then Brooks came and held her in his arms. Jackie's eyes closed and she relaxed in his embrace.

'Jackie, Jackie,' he murmured in her ear.

'Brooks.' She tilted her head back a little and held his face in her hands. 'Brooks, did you mean what you said before?'

'Absolutely.'

'Did you really mean it, without reservation?'

'You know I did.'

'Okay, let's talk about it,' Jackie said. She sat down in one of the armchairs and Brooks took the other. 'A wife my age might be a liability for a man entering politics. The newspapers will always be trying to make a story out of it and you could lose votes.'

Matthews was impressed that she had even raised this consideration, and at the same time he was touched that her first concern had been for him.

'I don't think that's a problem,' he said. 'It hasn't hurt Pierre Trudeau or Senator Strom Thurmond. And in Utah it really isn't going to matter at all. A lot of the Mormons have pretty unusual marriages of their own, you know.'

'Okay, what about me? I'd like to finish college.'

'Of course,' Matthews agreed. 'We have some very fine colleges and universities in Utah and I'm sure you could transfer with no difficulty. You may not like the idea of leaving New London and that's a decision you have to make for yourself. But I love you and I want you with me.'

Jackie thought about that for a minute, then put it aside for future contemplation. If she wanted to marry Brooks, college was really a secondary issue that could be worked out one way or another.

'If . . . if we married—' it seemed so strange to say it aloud for the first time!—'when would you see it happening?'

'The sooner the better, as far as I'm concerned,' Brooks said without hesitation. 'If we tried to carry on, too far apart for too long a time, well, I'd be afraid of losing you, Jackie.'

'I need time. I don't know how much, but I do need some time.'

'I understand. Any way you want it, I'm willing to go along and do whatever I can to make it work.'

'I want to, Brooks, I really do want to, but this is so fast.'

'I know, don't worry.'

'Brooks, can we be—engaged?' When Matthews immediately broke into a happy grin Jackie saw the implication in her question, and she added shyly, 'I guess I'm saying yes. Yes.' It felt good. She smiled.

'I'll come back here as often as I can to see you,' Matthews assured her, 'and we'll keep the telephone wires hot. But it has to be secret, Jackie, at least for now. If the press gets a hold of the fact that I'm courting a college girl, that I'm engaged to her—well, you can imagine what that would be like. Photographers on our heels every minute of the day. It'd kill us. It has to be secret, until we're married.'

Jackie nodded. The only person she would tell was Sandy, whom she knew she could trust. Aunt Josie —Jackie wouldn't tell her until later, when she was sure and ready for the marriage to take place. Jackie knew that the gossip press could ruin things for her and Brooks if they slipped up at all. Their relationship should fly or fall on its own, uninfluenced by anything outside of them. Right now she was just a student, but Brooks had a lot at stake—which was one reason why she admired the courage of his proposal. When the time came for him to announce his candidacy and the campaign began, Jackie wanted to be there, not just a pretty face but a working partner. It was a great opportunity. She could learn so much, expand her knowledge of the issues and make a real contribution as an actively involved, intelligent person in her own right. That could only help Brooks. She would not be happy with the dumb role of a candidate's bland wife, incapable of anything more serious than a woman's page chat on her husband's favourite dishes. Jackie had more to offer than that.

'The press won't learn about it from my side,' Jackie said. 'But they know you—maybe you'd better start putting together some disguises.'

Matthews laughed. 'It might come to that.' He lifted Jackie from her seat and carried her to the bed. 'A gorgeous creature like you with nothing on but an overcoat—too much.'

He sat down beside her on the bed, pulled the coat open and teased her nipples with the palm of his hand. Her fingers played lightly with the hair on his forearm. She looked up at him from the pillow, her face at once full of love but startlingly vulnerable.

'Brooks . . .'

'Mmmmn?'

'You know what I don't understand?'

'What?'

'Why me?'

'Hmmn?'

'Why me?'

'Jackie.' Brooks leaned over and nuzzled her neck and ear in a way that sent a lovely tingling feeling down her legs.

'I mean it, Brooks,' she said. 'I have to know. It's important. After all this time you've been alone, all the women you've met . . . suddenly you choose me. Why?'

Matthews looked at her and sighed. 'Jackie, I love you, what more can I say? I can't explain that, I just know it's happening and it's right. If it wasn't right it wouldn't be happening. Don't you think it's just as much a surprise to me as it is to you?'

Jackie gazed at his eyes, losing herself as she always did in their vibrant depths. 'You really love me,' she whispered so softly the sound barely left her throat. 'Yes . . . yes . . . don't please don't hurt me.'

They made love violently, tearing at each other in a frenzy, like two people clawing after some hidden truth the body could reveal. They fought like two young animals struggling for dominance, first one charging and forcing, then the other wrestling the lead away. It was as if they had both tacitly agreed to cut that last mental anchor and to let themselves sail into a final, uncharted sea. They became selfish, punishing and abusive, a man and a woman caught up in an overwhelming sensual fury. Finally they lay quiescent side by side, panting, slightly awed, staring at each other with respect and wonderment, as if they had both passed some impossible test together.

SEVEN

♦

It stopped snowing as the day dawned; a light, powdery dusting that, for a few hours anyway, transformed the city of Philadelphia. Jackie was up early, in time to see the last flurries sail to earth. An image from childhood surfaced briefly in her mind and she knew again the magic and excitement a fresh snowfall can bring. Everything looked beautiful and the world was still. It was a good omen, she thought. The perfect start to a new year, and a new life.

January one. Jackie could hardly believe the time had gone so fast, two and a half months flown by. So well, so wonderfully well. Her initial doubts had all been erased, systematically, comprehensively. She remembered a joking remark Sandy had made back at the beginning, about Matthews flying east from Utah every week-end to see Jackie. But he had very nearly done just that: four trips in seven weeks, and his latest (and last) visit had begun the week before Christmas. Jackie worked it out that they had been together for twenty-nine of the seventy-eight days since they first met.

Not a bad average, she thought. Is a cumulative

month enough time for two people to learn all they need to know about each other, to prove to themselves that their relationship is sound? In this case Jackie was certain that it was. She cherished the vivid memories of those seventy-eight days, the whirlwind visits and the marathon phone calls that came almost nightly in between. Yes, Brooks had proved himself, far beyond a shadow of a doubt. He was an amazing and wonderful man.

They had met in New York again twice. With Brooks, the city that had always daunted her a little became their toy, a dazzling playground that they explored and used as if it had been built solely for their delight. That was only one of many special things about Brooks—the way he could make the world so much more real and personal and alive to Jackie. Truly she felt like a person coming out of a long, long daydream, that she was finally growing up. Brooks had taken charge of her life, and was making a woman out of her.

On two other occasions they met at LaGuardia Airport, hired a car and drove up into the hills of northern Connecticut. They stayed at a different country inn each night, soaked up the splendid landscape and the dying beauty of its flamboyant autumn colours, prowled antique shops and old book barns, and spent a great many hours together in bed.

College, her other life, became a receding blur that held less and less relevance. It would soon be over and gone for good.

She and Sandy had, of course, talked about the situation and Jackie's plans day after day until it seemed they should have exhausted the subject twice over—and still they talked. Jackie didn't mind. Sandy was her best friend, her only true friend, and Jackie was eager to convince her.

Initially Sandy wouldn't believe anything: that Jackie was really serious about Brooks and vice-versa, that it would last until Christmas, that Jackie honestly didn't mind the fact that he was more than twice her age, and so on. But Sandy soon began to appreciate that they were not just fooling around, and that worried her. Was Jackie throwing herself away on a ridiculous crush, and if so what should she, Sandy, do about it? Or was the relationship, miraculously, good? So good as to merit Jackie's leaving college and getting married? Jackie talked about transferring to a university in Utah but Sandy knew that her friend was not taking any steps to bring about such a move. Jackie seemed to have lost all interest in her studies.

Sandy had argued that Jackie wasn't giving herself a chance. There was plenty of time to meet new people, go places, get a degree, think about a job and a career—before jumping into marriage. Why voluntarily deprive herself of all that? But Jackie countered that she had something so good and so precious that she would be a fool to risk letting it slip away. Nor was she depriving herself of anything; with Brooks she would probably go more places, meet more interesting people, see and do far more than she otherwise would.

'He's a real star,' Sandy remarked once.

'Believe it,' Jackie said, oblivious to the edge in her friend's voice.

'What about ten or twelve years from now, when you're still a young and attractive woman and he's starting to lay in stocks of Geritol?'

'San-dy, don't be silly.'

'I'm not. Listen, it's a simple fact. He's going to be sailing into his Golden Years at a time when you've still got everything going for you. That's not going to be easy. How are you going to cope with it?'

'You could have said the same thing to Lauren Bacall when she married Humphrey Bogart,' Jackie pointed out. 'Go ask her if she thinks she made a mistake.'

'Oh, Jackie, now you're being silly.'

Jackie shook her head. 'I love the man, Sandy, it's

that simple. His getting older isn't going to change that.'

'I don't know.'

'Besides, Brooks is not the sort of man who would ever reach a certain age and decide, that's it, I'm an Old Person now. He keeps in shape, he works out, doesn't smoke, and he leads a very active life. He'll be livelier at seventy-five than a lot of suburbanites are in their thirties.'

'I hope so,' Sandy said.

As the days and weeks passed, Sandy's worries gradually diminished. They never entirely disappeared, but by Christmas, they seemed to be nothing more than the usual hopes and fears one has when a person close to them is about to marry. More than anything, Sandy was persuaded by the visible change taking place in Jackie. She carried herself with more purpose and confidence, a person who now knew who she was and where she was going. She seemed brighter, almost aglow at times, and undeniably happier. You can't argue against that, Sandy realized.

'You can't sleep, can you?'

Jackie turned from the window and the snowy vista outside.

'Morning, Aunt Josie,' she said. 'I woke up early. Have you seen the snow?'

'Yes, it's lovely, and not too much of it.' The old woman crossed the small parlour in a few steps and sat by Jackie. 'You can't sleep,' she repeated, smiling kindly.

'I got about three hours, but I don't feel tired.'

'Not yet you don't. Three hours?'

'Sandy and I sat up late talking. We must have covered every single thing we've ever done together and everyone we know—real roomie stuff.' Jackie smiled a little sadly. 'It was nice.'

'That's good.' Aunt Josie regarded her niece. 'Do you feel all right—you didn't drink too much after I went to bed, did you?'

Jackie laughed gently. 'It was New Year's Eve, don't forget. I feel fine.'

'Even so.'

Brooks had taken Jackie, Sandy and Aunt Josie out to dinner, along with the Parmenters, a middle-aged couple from the University of Pennsylvania whom Brooks was staying with in town. Afterwards they had returned to Aunt Josie's house to see in the New Year with champagne.

'They're nice people,' Jackie said. 'The Parmenters.'

Ignoring that, Aunt Josie said, 'This is my favourite time of the day.'

'I know,' Jackie said. 'You always did get up with the sun, didn't you?'

'It's a good time of day to sit and think.'

Jackie could see it coming now. Aunt Josie had been harder to persuade than Sandy. Maybe she would never fully come round to the idea of Jackie marrying Brooks. Although Aunt Josie didn't argue with Jackie, she made her displeasure clear by what she didn't say, and a general lack of enthusiasm. She didn't like the age difference, Jackie knew from the way her aunt had winced when first told. Also, she did make one remark which suggested that all lawyers were suspect in her book. But what bothered Aunt Josie most, Jackie believed, was Utah. Jackie would be so far away and the old woman left to use up the rest of her time alone.

Aunt Josie had warmed a little to Brooks over the holidays, going from cool civility to tepid cordiality, but she was past the stage where charm counted for much. She had to give Brooks credit for being neither patronizing nor evasive with her. He had made a point of coming to speak privately with Aunt Josie shortly after he had arrived in town, and he didn't waste time with awkward pleasantries.

'I'm sure you were surprised when Jackie told you about us,' he said.

'I was.'

'And angry perhaps, and worried,' Brooks went on. 'I can understand all the fears and misgivings you might have, Aunt Josie, and I know I can't erase them overnight. But I do want you to know that I'm deeply in love with Jackie, I really am, and I promise you we're not making a mistake.'

'Everyone thinks that when they're getting married.'

'I know, but I'm not a fresh-faced kid any more. I've had my ups and downs like anyone else, and I've made my share of mistakes. But I'd like to think that I've learned from them.'

'Mr Matthews,' Aunt Josie said stiffly, 'why did you choose my niece? Why Jackie?'

Brooks smiled tightly. 'That's the way it happened,' he said. 'I didn't choose her, as such. We met and our feelings for each other grew naturally. We're right for each other. In my line of work I meet a great many people, professionally and socially, but no one has ever come close to making me feel the way I do about Jackie. When that happens, you *know* it's right.'

The elderly woman sighed. Matthews seemed sincere, and he obviously wasn't afraid to talk to her. But she reminded herself that he was a lawyer. Talk was his business. He could probably talk like this all day, sounding mature, candid and plausible—but did it really mean anything?

'She is so young, Mr Matthews, and innocent.'

'In many ways she is innocent,' Brooks agreed promptly. 'I think that's one of the reasons I love her so much. The last thing I'd ever want to do is damage that quality, which is so rare in people today. But that doesn't mean she doesn't know what she's doing. Jackie's very bright and she's an adult. She's not the kind of person who would take a step like this lightly.'

That was exactly what Aunt Josie would have liked to believe about Jackie, but . . .

'Aunt Josie, the only thing that'll put your mind at

ease is to see us happy together,' Brooks said. 'To see that the marriage is good and does work. We're going to fly you out to Utah to spend some time with us in a few months, when the winter's over. You can stay with us as long as you want. Reserve final judgement until then, and I think you'll feel a lot better about it.'

Aunt Josie nodded briefly. But, she thought, if it really is a big mistake it will be far too late then.

Now, on the first day of January, the day on which Jackie and Brooks were to be wed, Aunt Josie struggled with herself. She desperately wanted Jackie to be happy, and if the girl had made her choice it would be wrong to try and stand in the way or spoil things. But she had raised Jackie from a tot of three to womanhood. She felt uneasy about this marriage and this moment, she realized glumly, was probably her last chance to say something.

'Sit close to me, Jackie,' she said. 'Takes me longer to warm up every day.'

Jackie joined her aunt on the sofa and hugged her. 'How about if I make you a nice pot of tea?'

'In a few minutes,' Aunt Josie said. 'Let's just sit like this for now.'

'Fine.'

'Are you all right, child? Are you really all right?'

'Yes, Aunt Josie.'

'Scared at all?'

'No. A little nervous maybe, and excited.'

'That's natural,' the old woman said, gazing out the window at the snow and the gathering daylight.

'You don't have to worry about me, Aunt Josie. I know you do, but—'

'Are you sure, child?'

'Yes.'

'About him, are you sure?'

'Oh yes.'

'A little more time would—'

'No.' The word was spoken quietly but it seemed to

fill the room. 'The time is now and I know it's right.'

They sat there for a long time, holding each other without speaking. It was as if they were both trying to memorize something shared, a feeling or a single moment or a lifetime, a beautiful and luminous period that now, each knew, was over.

Finally Jackie rose and went to the kitchen where she occupied herself making a pot of tea. We're almost changing roles, she thought, placing two cups on a tray. For all those years, Aunt Josie was the one who was always there when needed, the person who helped me, taught me, comforted me. After today, though, Jackie knew it would be up to her to look after Aunt Josie, to make sure that she never felt neglected or unloved.

'Strong and hot,' Jackie announced as she brought the tea tray into the parlour.

'Thank you, dear.' Aunt Josie hadn't moved from the sofa.

'After I'm settled in there, you are coming out for a good long visit,' Jackie said cheerfully.

'To Utah?' A lifelong east coast city-dweller, Aunt Josie found it hard to imagine life beyond the Mississippi.

'Of course. It's beautiful country out there. You might even like it enough to stay.'

'Utah,' Aunt Josie said dubiously.

The wedding was short, simple and secret. Jackie had agreed with Brooks that it would be better that way. He found a Justice of the Peace who was happy to have his New Year's Day interrupted briefly for the customary fee. George Parmenter was Brooks's best man and Sandy was Jackie's maid of honour. Mrs Parmenter took pictures. Aunt Josie didn't cry but she came close, eyes brimming and glistening. The JP's wife stood to one side, smiling benignly, as if she had seen this ceremony thousands of times but was never bored by it. The JP himself was much more matter-of-fact about it all, moving steadily through the text like a man calling out the items on a stocklist.

After a lavish lunch at a restaurant, the wedding party returned to Aunt Josie's house where the champagne continued to flow. A couple of Aunt Josie's neighbours came by, people Jackie had known since she was a child. It was a small but festive gathering, full of good cheer. Jackie was loving every minute of it and, seeing her so happy, Aunt Josie banished her own doubts.

When the afternoon began to lengthen towards evening, Jackie went upstairs to change. She hadn't bothered to wear a long wedding-gown and veil, but had chosen instead a simple, elegant dress. She packed it carefully and put on a trouser suit. As she was brushing her hair, Sandy entered the room. They hugged each other, smiling through the tears.

'He better be good to you,' Sandy said.

'He already is. I'll phone you every week, and you're coming out to stay with us this summer, remember.'

'You look glorious,' Sandy said. 'Oh, Jackie, I'm so happy for you.'

Brooks put their suitcases in the rented Mercedes and after many more hugs and goodbyes all around they were ready to leave.

Aunt Josie, who had disappeared a moment earlier, now reappeared. She and Jackie embraced.

'This is for you,' the elder woman said quietly, pressing a small object in Jackie's hand.

'Oh, it's beautiful.'

The antique locket held an old and faded picture of a woman that looked as if it had been hurriedly cut out of a larger photograph.

'That's your great-aunt Charlotte. Of course you never knew her but she was a fine woman. She ran away with a man when she was only sixteen.'

'Really?'

'Yes, and they were happy together the rest of their lives.'

'Oh, Aunt Josie, thank you.'

'God bless you, child.'

'Thank you. Thank you for—for everything, for my life. I love you.'

2
UNION

EIGHT

◆

Martha Raeburn couldn't believe it. She kept telling herself it was a joke, that it wasn't true. Twice that morning at school she actually emptied her handbag and searched through its contents for her car keys. Of course they weren't there. She knew very well that her father had taken them away from her at breakfast, but the fact still defied belief. By lunchtime she was finally forced to admit to a friend, 'You know, the dumb fuck did it, he really went and did it. He took away my car.'

For two weeks, no less. That was what hurt the most. If it had been for a day or two, Martha could sulk and live through it, but two whole weeks—that was crazy, impossible. And for what? She hadn't even done anything wrong. When she got home last night: the Big Scene. She wasn't late, but her father seemed to go berserk, yelling that he could smell grass on her, that she had been out smoking drugs and doing God-only-knows-what with criminals and degenerates. Martha was stunned. Sure, she had smoked joints and taken other drugs on occasion in the past, and sex was certainly not unknown to her. But last night was strictly a non-event. She and her girl-friend had driven around for a couple of hours, but nothing much was happening in town and so they'd gone home early. Then, there was the old man, blaming her for just about everything since Pearl Harbor. It was too much. He's really flipped this time, Martha thought.

At breakfast, Judgement was passed. She came to the table to find him dangling the car keys over his bowl of cornflakes. He put them in his pocket and announced the two-week penalty. For good measure he told Martha he had removed the distributor cap from her car and hidden it. She and her father screamed at each other for ten minutes or so, while her brother Ralph calmly read the sports pages, and then Martha stormed off to school.

Disbelief turned to rage. He can't do this to me, Martha told herself over and over again. I'm eighteen, not a child. Besides, I didn't even do anything to deserve this. Past offences, which her father knew nothing about, didn't apply, she reasoned. That was probably it, too: the fact that he had never actually been able to catch her at any wrongdoing, and now his suspicious imagination had finally boiled over. Well, he wasn't going to get away with it. One way or another, she'd show him.

This kind of trouble had started a couple of years ago, shortly after Martha's mother had died of a heart attack. Bill Raeburn was deeply shaken by the sudden, unexpected loss of his wife. He seemed to become abrupt and arbitrary about everything, and he began to act as if he were determined that Martha, his daughter and the only female left in his life, would never grow up. He showered her with exaggerated affection and gifts, like the car, but it was impossible for Martha to feel anything other than contempt. He was keeping her on a short leash and she knew it. He simply couldn't accept the fact that she was a young woman, a person in her own right who had come of age. Every effort he made to lock Martha more tightly into his illusion of a timeless family life, only succeeded in driving her further away emotionally. She could still feel pity for her father sometimes, but now even that was fast disappearing. She seldom gave the matter any thought because as far as she was concerned there wasn't much to think about. It was too late for her father, there was nothing she could do for him the way he was. She had her own life to consider, and she was not going to let him ruin it. What she feared most was being kept as his little prisoner for the next twenty or thirty years. No way was she going to stand by and allow that to happen.

The rage simmered in Martha for hours. By the time school finished that day she was ready to do something—she didn't know what, but she had to do something. It would have to hurt him in the same way that he was hurting her. It might bring down his wrath on her all over again, but that didn't matter. Maybe, just maybe, if she did it right, the message might get through to him. *Lay off me, I'm not your little baby girl any more.* Martha had no real hope that anything she did would make her father see the light. She was sure he was beyond that now, but she was going to do something anyway, for her own personal satisfaction if nothing else. She didn't bother taking the bus, choosing instead to march the two miles home, letting the fury mount within her every step of the way.

When she reached the house, Martha stood looking at it for a moment. An ordinary raised ranch on an ordinary residential street. For years it had been her home, but now it seemed strange, alien, as if it were no longer hers and never had been—or rather, that she didn't belong to it any more. It. Him. What was she going to do—smash a window, throw dishes around in the kitchen or get drunk on her father's brandy and write obscenities on the walls? No, a better idea presented itself to her. On the front lawn was that kitchy statue of a Negro jockey. They used to be quite common in the gardens of white American homes. In recent years many people had quietly stashed them away in basements or garages, but that idea had never occurred to Bill Raeburn.

Martha went into the house, threw down her schoolbooks and then descended the stairs to her father's workshop in the basement. She grabbed the first hammer she saw and hurried back outside. She swung the tool as hard as she could, pounding away chunks of the jockey statue. It was hard work, and Martha was half-shouting, half-gasping with each strike. *Damn you, damn you, damn you.* Chips flew through the air. The statue was made of some kind of tough cement or plaster, but it was breaking up. In a few minutes Martha had reduced the head to an unrecognizable lump of rubble, and she started in on the arms and shoulders. *Damn you, damn you, damn you . . .*

Mrs Soderholm, the widow who lived in the next house, came out on to her front step, one hand pressed anxiously to her throat. She glanced around, looking for another witness to this strange act, but no one else was around at the moment.

'Martha. Martha, be careful, you're damaging that,' she said absurdly. 'Did your father tell you to do that? I don't think he did.'

Martha snarled something unintelligible.

'Are you all right, Martha? Are you?'

'Mind your own business, you old fool,' Martha hollered back.

Mrs Soderholm stiffened. 'The nerve of that rude little brat,' she said to herself. The elderly woman retreated back into her house with a shudder. She'd have to put up with them screaming at each other again tonight. All three of those Raeburns had been going to the dogs ever since the poor mother passed away. Perhaps it was time to think about moving.

The handle of the hammer cracked, and on the next blow it shattered completely. Martha threw it aside disgustedly and sat down on the lawn. Idly, she picked at pieces of debris from the statue. Then she had to struggle to hold back the tears. *Damn, damn, damn it all anyway* . . . She was exhausted and sweating but she tried to revive her anger. It was the only refuge she knew.

'Wow.'

Martha looked up. A dusty, old, powder-blue convertible had pulled over to the kerb.

'What the hell are you looking at?' she snapped.

'That thing,' the young man behind the wheel said, nodding to the battered remains of the jockey. 'You sure did a number on that little feller.'

'What's it to you?'

'Nothin', only I just hate to see an unhappy woman, that's all, and you look pretty unhappy.'

Maybe it was the use of the word 'woman' that made Martha look up at the young man again. He was kind of handsome, with a nice smile, even if he did drive a clunker.

'Get lost,' she said, but there was no edge in her voice.

'Aw, you're mad, but it's not me you're mad at, is it? Tell you what, why don't we take a ride down the road, maybe get a burger and somethin' nice to wash it down with? Nothin' like a nice drive with the breeze in your hair to make a person feel better.'

Martha studied the young man. A picture formed in her mind: she and this stranger were inside on the couch making out passionately when her father comes through the door. That'd hit him, right in his own house. But he wouldn't be home from work for maybe another three hours, and besides, she'd done enough here already. Martha stood up and walked to the car. Well, she thought, if I can't use my car . . . She got in on the passenger side and sat back without saying a word. They drove off.

'Father or mother?' the young man asked after they had gone a couple of blocks.

'Father.'

'A pain, huh?'

'A pain? Yeah, a pain all right, and a sexist, racist, stupid son of a bitch . . .'

'All that?'

'That's the least of it. He . . . he's . . .' Martha shut her eyes, unable to say any more.

They drove for a while in silence. Martha was working her way into a good mood. She prided herself on being the kind of person who could do something without brooding about it endlessly thereafter. She had smashed up her father's lawn jockey pretty thoroughly, and she could see no point in worrying about it now. She certainly wasn't sorry she had done it. Now she was out for a ride with some guy and she was determined to enjoy herself, not to let thoughts of her father spoil the rest of the afternoon.

'Where are we going?' she asked.

'Wherever you want, babe,' the driver replied. 'You got any place special you want to go, you just say so.'

'Let's just cruise around,' Martha said after a moment's consideration. 'Okay?'

'Okay by me.'

'He really thinks I'm still his little baby girl, you know,' Martha said. 'He treats me like a child all the time. He's either cooing around me like some goddamn sick pigeon, or else he's blowing his top because I haven't done something exactly the way he wants it. He's—shit, listen to me, I'm still talking about him. You see how screwed up he's got me? He bugs me even when he's not around.'

'Yeah, parents need a lot of educatin' when it comes to handlin' their kids,' the young man said with a smile. 'Best thing for you to do is not let him get you so all riled up, because if you do that means he's winning and—'

'How can I do that when he's on my back all the time?'

'Hold your own but don't be so quick to fight him over every little thing. I believe you've got a bit of a temper, right? Now that's okay, but you got to know when to use it, when not to, and with your old man you got to remember that time is on your side, not his. He knows he's losin' you and there ain't a thing he can do about it. 'Course he'll try, because he's scared and alone and worried that any day now you'll pack up and go. Do you understand what I'm telling you?'

'Yeah . . .' Martha was surprised that this young man, who was a complete stranger, could talk to her as if he had known her and her family for years.

'You'll make it, he won't. That's the law of life, and if you can remember that and keep a bit of self-confidence all the time, well, then I think you'll find it gets easier day by day.'

'Maybe you're right,' Martha said. She turned slightly on the car seat to look at the driver. He looked young enough to be fresh out of high school, but you could tell he had been around, and had seen and done things most boys hadn't. He had the calm, assured air of a person who knew who he was and did his own thing.

'I bet you don't take shit from anybody,' Martha said.

'I try not to,' the young man said, smiling broadly again.

'I don't know if it'll do any good, but I'll think about what you said.' Martha liked this fellow. He talked to her as if she were an intelligent adult. Whenever she moaned about her father to any of the boys at school, they just moaned right back about their parents, never having anything useful to say ('You're Daddy's girl, you should be able to wrap him around your little finger,' was the height of their analytical abilities).

'You do that,' the young man said. 'You'll see, there's more than one way to sit on a pain in the ass.'

Martha laughed and felt completely at ease with this man. They talked some more and joked, and she let her skirt slide a few inches above her knees.

Martha told him about school and her friends, and such was the depth of her self-absorption that she scarcely asked the driver a single question about himself. He listened attentively, smiling that smile of his and throwing in humorous comments from time to time.

For more than an hour they drove around town, circling gradually away from the centre. They turned on to a narrow road that ran into a forest and, a mile along it, they pulled over by a large pond. The only sound was that of a light breeze in the trees and the distant hammering of a woodpecker.

'I'm not from around here,' the young man volunteered. 'What is this place?'

'This is the local Rod and Gun Club,' Martha answered.

'Oh yeah? They do a lot of huntin' and fishin' here?'

'Mostly they get blasted at the clubhouse bar.'

'Where's that?'

'About five miles down the road, on the other side of that hill at the end of the pond.'

The young man got out of the car and rummaged around in a box on the floor of the back seat, finally coming up with two bottles of beer.

'Want one?' he asked.

'Sure.'

'They warmed up some but I didn't think it was a good idea to drink them while we were driving around in town.'

After he opened the bottle and gave it to Martha, the young man turned away from her and strolled twenty yards to the edge of the pond. Martha watched him, and then got out of the car to follow.

'It's pretty here,' he said almost to himself. 'Real pretty, isn't it?'

Martha held back a few steps and said nothing. When the young man glanced back to find her, she smiled at him. He saw that she had undone the third and fourth buttons on her blouse.

'Come here,' he said.

When she stood only inches from him, he touched her hair, her cheek and then her breast. Martha was excited, not at all nervous. She hadn't realized how tall he was, nor how deep and beautiful his eyes were. Gently, he opened her blouse and bent down to kiss her left breast. Martha's arms were coming round to embrace him just as the blade slid in and up.

'Oh yes . . . Oh yes,' he whispered, holding her until her gasping, fluttering movements ceased.

Then he got on with it.

They would find Martha Raeburn's body near the side of the road there. In one hand would be her head, and in the other, her heart.

NINE
◆

Jackie was staggered by the beauty of Utah. She had expected it to be different, better than the vague images she had in mind, but she wasn't prepared for the awesome range of its features. The Matthews house was located in the town of Cleary Centre, which had probably started out as nothing more than a crossroads stop half-way between Salt Lake City and Provo, but now had grown into an attractive little community. Just to the west the austere but vivid Great Salt Lake Desert began, while immediately to the east the powerful Uinta Mountains rose up more than two miles above sea level. With the Great Salt Lake itself just north and Utah Lake a short drive south, Jackie realized that her new home was in an astonishing focal point of the land, a place where some of the earth's most dramatic features converged.

Jackie liked the house immediately; its neocolonial style and layout reminded her of the north-east where she had grown up, and made her feel completely comfortable. The house had been built shortly after World War II and Brooks was only its second owner. He had bought it and the three lovely acres around it at the time of his first marriage. He told Jackie that after the second marriage broke up, he had decided stubbornly that this was his home, he liked it and he saw no reason to move to smaller, more suitable bachelor quarters.

'And now, after all this time, I'm proved right,' he said proudly. 'You're here.'

In addition to the master bedroom, the house had three other bedrooms—once obviously intended for children. And there would be children, Jackie thought happily. She was pleased that Brooks had never let the house go, holding on to it for so many years when he was its sole occupant. Now the place would come alive with love at last.

If the Matthews home had any drawback, it was a minor one. The view in all directions was excellent, but high on a hill a couple of miles away was Rabar Penitentiary, a dour grey smudge on the landscape which could be seen from the back garden and two upstairs windows.

'I bet this summer we can figure out exactly the right spot for a lovely great oak tree, that would blot out that place without destroying the rest of the view,' Jackie said.

'You think you can move around a fully grown oak like it was a tomato plant?' Brooks asked with amusement.

'Well, maybe a fir. We'll think of something.'

'Maybe.'

'Even if we had to wait a while for it to grow, that would be okay. I just don't like seeing that place over there.'

'I know,' said Brooks, 'but it made sense to the previous owner. The house was originally built for the prison governor, and I guess he wanted to be able to keep an eye on his work at all times. It only came on to the market when they built another house for the governor, nearer the prison, and I just happened to be around at the right time, and bought it.'

'It's a terrific house and I love it. I just wish—this sounds really dumb—that it had nothing to do with that place . . . the way it sits there, it's almost as if it were watching us, not the other way round. But this time next year—when I've planted that tree—it will be perfect. And I do love it, Brooks, I really do.'

Their honeymoon had been fun as well as romantic and pleasurable. Brooks and Jackie had driven from Philadelphia into the countryside, stopping for the night at a sleepy hotel just across the Maryland line. The next day they proceeded into Washington, where they spent the rest of the week either sightseeing or in bed.

'There's an interesting property,' Brooks deadpanned as they drove past the White House. 'We might think about it some time when it comes vacant.'

'I hear the plumbing's lousy,' Jackie joked back, but at the same time she felt a tiny thrill, knowing that she was now married to a man who in the next ten years or so might well become a serious presidential contender.

From Washington they flew down to Nassau where they luxuriated in the sun for another full week, swimming, walking the beaches and dining on the likes of crawfish and yellow bird at the Balmoral Beach Hotel. Jackie felt perfectly comfortable with Brooks. He had a good body and looked younger than he was. At first Jackie had watched carefully, expecting some disapproving glances to come their way, but none did that she could see and she soon forgot about it, losing that trace of self-consciousness.

By the time they made the long journey to Utah, they were a little travel-weary but otherwise rested, refreshed and very happy. Brooks was returning to familiar territory, but to Jackie it was a new adventure. The moment she saw the house it felt right, and she laughed merrily when Brooks carried her across the threshold.

The first few months sped by and with the advent of spring, Jackie felt that she had well and truly settled into her new home. She had met many of Brooks's local friends and colleagues, all of whom gave cocktail parties or dinners for the expressed purpose of meeting the new bride. It was a curious but not unpleasant experience, being more or less on show for the first weeks, but most of those she was introduced to were friendly and relaxed, so Jackie soon overcame her initial shyness. She especially liked Larry Sterling and Mel Dyson, two men in their middle thirties who worked with Brooks and were devoted to him. As far as Jackie could tell, no one she met regarded her critically or suspiciously. She wouldn't have been surprised if some of Brooks's friends, motivated by nothing other than honest concern for him, had looked on her coldly as an opportunist taking advantage of a lonely man, but this did not happen. Larry and Mel even went so far as to take Jackie aside and tell her how delighted they were that Brooks had finally married again, and that they were sure she would be good for him.

From the beginning, Jackie watched Brooks carefully, eager to make sure that they adjusted to living together fulltime as smoothly as possible. She didn't want to disrupt any important personal habits or ways he might have grown accustomed to over twenty years of being on his own. Jackie wanted to fit in the home with a minimum of fuss, letting her part develop naturally without pushing herself too fast and too soon. Brooks seemed very happy.

Much of the time he was engrossed in the hunt for The Blade, the shadowy, unknown killer who remained at large. Seldom would two days in succession pass without Jackie hearing some mention of that horrible nickname. Brooks was one of the people who kept applying pressure to the police force. He consulted with them on a weekly basis, badgering them with phone calls in between meetings, to make sure that everything that could be done was in fact being done. He stayed abreast of every move in the hunt, and felt free to call one official or another at any time of the day or night, to raise a query or offer a new idea. Listening to him in action sometimes, Jackie was impressed by his ability to harangue, cajole, flatter and berate a person, all in the space of a few minutes and always, apparently, to good effect. Brooks Matthews had undeniable and formidable skills when it came to dealing with people. Jackie looked forward to the day when he would be able to put them to use in the sphere of politics. But it was typical of the man that he would tackle first things first, and he was going all out to bring the case against The Blade to its proper conclusion as promptly as possible.

That first Sunday morning they had spent together in New York last October, after Larry Sterling's telephone call and a furious love-making session, Brooks had related to Jackie the basic details of The Blade's crimes. Nothing more had happened in the three months that followed but then, shortly after Brooks and Jackie arrived in Utah from their honeymoon, the killer struck again. A girl of seventeen was found dead, her body bearing the gruesome signs of The Blade's handiwork. It had happened just outside Coalville, a town close enough to give Jackie an uneasy, creepy feeling.

'It won't be long now,' Brooks said reassuringly at the time. 'Psychopaths like that get caught up in a rhythm that accelerates faster and faster until something finally gives and they either destroy themselves or make the kind of mistakes that soon land them in jail.'

'I hope so,' Jackie said fervently.

'We'll have him, and soon. I can feel it, I just know we'll get that boy before too much longer. And when we do, after what he's done and the way people feel, it'll be the chair for him.'

'The electric chair?'

'For sure.'

But in spite of Brooks's optimism the rest of January, all of February and March passed by without any further developments in the case. Jackie could see that Brooks was growing increasingly perplexed and frustrated.

'Maybe he's just gone away,' Jackie said hopefully.

Brooks smiled indulgently. 'That would be nice, but life is seldom that convenient,' he said. 'No, he's still out there somewhere.'

But if The Blade was an unpleasant fact of life for the time being, he did not interfere with the happiness Brooks and Jackie shared. She took to her new home and new surroundings easily. Brooks was working at the peak of his energy, handling the daily flow of his regular legal work and monitoring the search for The Blade, but he never let it disrupt his home life. He didn't neglect Jackie and he wouldn't carry a bad mood into his time with her.

In April the stark beauty of the land erupted in new growth. Jackie could see that before too long the place would transform itself into a kind of lush and colourful oasis, a small but miraculous area between the inhospitable desert and the forbidding mountains. She could understand why the Mormons must have thought they had found Paradise when, in the last century, they had first crossed some of the bleakest and most dangerous parts of America to find this spot.

Jackie took a driving course and duly passed the tests to get her licence. It was something she had never bothered with in Philadelphia or at college, not having much need or opportunity to drive. But living in Cleary Centre, Utah, was a different matter, and she couldn't be housebound, dependent on others to get around. Once she gained a sense of confidence handling a car, Jackie loved driving. Brooks, always generous, bought her a Thunderbird. Jackie made a point of getting out every day, even if only for a few minutes, to perfect her driving skills—and just to enjoy the great freedom of roaming around.

Brooks was so generous, in fact, that Jackie felt she had to resist gently sometimes. 'You'll make me lazy and spoiled,' she would say. She was not yet a very knowledgeable cook, for instance, and Brooks's long bachelor existence had given him a liking for restaurant food. So she gradually brought him around to the idea that they should eat at home most of the time, rather than dining out so much. Jackie was pleased: she was learning how to be a good cook and at the same time she was strengthening their home life in a small but not insignificant way.

Jackie never took the matter of her college studies any further. Aunt Josie was unhappy about this, she knew, but the simple truth was that with each passing day, college seemed to have less and less point to her—when she thought about it at all. Jackie was a married woman now, with a husband and a home to fill her life. She didn't have to prove anything to herself by working for a university degree and as far as other people were concerned, Jackie was eager only to show them, day after day, that her marriage to Brooks was good and true. She was in the adult world now and liking it; student life no longer had any appeal, although she did miss her former roommate. Every Monday night, Jackie phoned Sandy and talked for up to an hour. Jackie liked hearing what her friend had done over the week-end just finished, tales of boys from New Haven, Hartford, Boston or Providence. In January, she had been especially amused to hear how startled Dan and Stuart were when they learned that Jackie had recently become Mrs Brooks Matthews.

Jackie always did the phoning because Brooks didn't mind what the monthly bills were and Sandy's finances were those of a typical student—slim at best. But one day Sandy placed a surprise call.

'Hi, are you pregnant yet?' It was Sandy's standard greeting.

'Hi. No—hey, what's up?'

'Oh, nothing. I just thought I'd call and wish you a happy anniversary. Of sorts.'

'What?' Jackie couldn't imagine what Sandy was talking about. 'What anniversary?'

'God, you're an old married woman already. Today is May first and you've been married exactly four months.'

Jackie laughed. 'Okay, you caught me, I admit it. I'll try the same thing on Brooks tonight.'

'You do that. How's it going?'

'Oh, fine. Just getting the garden sorted out. We'll have plenty of fresh vegetables when you get here. Oh, listen to this. The other day Brooks said we should go up to the cottage this coming week-end.'

'What cottage?'

'That's what I said. Typical Brooks, wouldn't you know. It turns out he owns a cottage on Flaming Gorge Lake, and a boat!'

'God. Pardon me, but where the hell is Flaming Whatsis Lake?'

They both exploded in laughter. 'I don't know, exactly,' Jackie said. 'The other side of the mountains, two or three hours away.'

'Well, it sounds like it might be nice.'

'He showed me some pictures and, Sandy, the place is beautiful. We'll have to go up there when you come out to visit.'

'How long has he had it?'

'Oh, years.'

'What did he do with it, I mean all that time when he wasn't married?'

'He likes to go there for a little fishing and to work on his papers. He deliberately hasn't put a phone in, so once he gets there no one can bother him.'

'Uh-hunh. Sounds good.'

They chatted for another ten minutes before hanging up. It was always good to talk with Sandy. She was tentatively scheduled to arrive in mid-July and stay with Brooks and Jackie for three weeks.

Maybe by then I will be pregnant, she thought, smiling at how everyone seemed to raise the subject when talking with somebody newly married. Oddly enough, she and Brooks had never discussed it, but there seemed to be an unspoken feeling between them that whatever happened would be all right. Jackie was on the pill and Brooks must know that from seeing the packets. Perhaps it was time to think about giving that up and letting nature take its own course. A child? Yes, she thought, not in a rush, but when it happens. And the first-born would have to be a son, for Brooks.

TEN

◆

'We're going to a barbecue in a little while with some friends and people Brooks knows at work,' Jackie said. She and Aunt Josie had been talking on the telephone for nearly fifteen minutes now—one of Jackie's surprise calls that always delighted the elderly woman.

'That's nice. And how is Brooks?'

'He's fine and he sends you his love,' Jackie said. 'It's good to see him taking a day off for a change. He's been working so hard lately.'

'Keeps him out a lot, does it?'

'Oh, he's around.' It was almost too casual and Jackie knew it didn't sound quite right. 'It's just that sometimes he has to be reminded to sit down and relax.'

'Yes.'

'Even on week-ends around the house, he'll be working in his study on a brief or some paper he's writing. Brooks isn't one to sit in front of a TV watching baseball and drinking beer all day.'

'Well, that's good,' Aunt Josie said. 'As long as, you

know, he does take some time off. Work isn't everything.'

'I know.'

At that moment Brooks walked past the telephone alcove where Jackie was sitting. She looked up at him and smiled. He raised his eyebrows and tapped his watch, and then Jackie noticed that he was dressed and ready to leave, while she was still in her shower robe. She nodded, understanding, at the same time trying to keep up with Aunt Josie, who was still talking. Brooks held up ten fingers and then disappeared around the corner.

Jackie wound up the conversation with her aunt and hurried upstairs to dress. 'Sorry, darling,' she called out to Brooks on the way. 'I won't be long.' It took her no time at all to put on a pair of snug white shorts, an expensive T-shirt and her tennis shoes. She brushed her hair and applied a few light touches of make-up. Good, she thought, studying herself in the full-length mirror; very good. Jackie grabbed a shoulder bag, her sunglasses and she was ready to go.

But, downstairs, Brooks regarded her with evident displeasure.

'What's the matter, honey?'

'You're not going like that.'

'Yes, why not?'

Brooks glared. 'Why not? You'll have the husbands leering and wise-cracking, and the wives sharpening their knives. That's why not.'

'Brooks, don't be silly. I look fine. I know most of those people, they're not like that.'

'You're not going looking like Lolita,' Brooks said with finality. 'Get changed, and hurry.'

'Well, what do you want me to wear?' Jackie asked, feeling hurt and annoyed.

'Some other top and some other bottom,' Brooks answered flatly. He turned away and made a show of looking for something in the newspaper.

Jackie trudged back upstairs. It was the first time

Brooks had ever reacted unfavourably to the way she dressed. Damn, damn, she grumbled, taking off her clothes and throwing them to the floor. Jackie stood by the window for a few moments, feeling hurt and angry.

A few miles away, on the far hilltop, Rabar Penitentiary stood out in the bright sunshine. To Jackie, it looked like an ugly fungus, a blight on an otherwise attractive landscape. Why did she let it bother her? It couldn't grow or spread, and yet it seemed to suggest that very potential to her. Whenever Jackie's eyes fell on the place she couldn't help but think of it as a deadly cancer cell waiting for the right moment to break loose and sweep across the surrounding countryside. She and Brooks really had to get some trees and solve the problem of the eyesore.

Jackie put on a bra, a summery cotton blouse and a pair of slightly longer, slightly looser Bermuda shorts. This has got to be acceptable, she thought, turning to a mirror. Not as good as she could look but all right, in an ordinary kind of way, Jackie decided. She had calmed down now. Perhaps Brooks was right. He knew the people who were going to be at the barbecue better than she did, and maybe there were some who would have been annoyed or offended by her other outfit. Perhaps, too, Brooks knew that he might begin to feel jealous if she looked too fetching and attracted too much attention from some of the other men there. If that's what he was thinking, it was really rather sweet of him, Jackie concluded, even if he had been a bit grumpy about it.

'Okay now?'

Brooks glanced up from his paper. 'That's better.'

The drive to Mel Dyson's house took about thirty minutes. Jackie rested one hand on his thigh, as she often did when they rode together, and tried to chat with him, but Brooks was unreceptive.

'There's a lot of holiday traffic on the road, Jackie,' he said stonily. 'Don't distract me.'

'Sorry.'

She sat back on her side of the front seat and stared ahead. It wasn't really the traffic, she knew. Brooks had grown tenser and edgier in the past month, especially since 10 May. That was the day The Blade claimed his seventh victim, a young dental assistant in the town of Duchesne, a relatively isolated spot south of the Uintas. It was just after supper when Brooks took the call in the kitchen. He had poured himself another coffee and Jackie was putting dishes in the dishwasher.

'Duchesne?' Brooks bellowed incredulously into the telephone. 'How the hell can a guy go into a town like that, kill someone in broad daylight and then go on his way without anybody noticing? Can you tell me that? It was the same in Hanksville and again at Beaver. Jesus Christ Almighty . . . He's hitting small towns and they still can't pick him up, or even get a make on his car.'

Jackie remembered that night for another reason too. She and Brooks hadn't made love since. Three weeks now. He came home from the office, ate and then stayed in the study until late, making phone calls, poring over reports, staring at that map of Utah dotted with seven red pins. He wasn't cold or unfriendly—it was just that his mind was always somewhere else. Jackie desperately hoped that this business of The Blade would soon be over so that Brooks could get back to leading a more normal life.

At the same time she wondered if she wasn't partly responsible. She didn't tell Brooks when she stopped taking the pill, but perhaps he had noticed. It seemed unlikely, he was so preoccupied, and he hadn't said anything to her about it.

Jackie was glad they were going to this barbecue. With any luck Brooks would come away from it more relaxed and in a better frame of mind for having put his work aside those few hours. Then perhaps, when they got home, Jackie and Brooks could have a long talk, in more ways than one.

A line of cars was parked along the road in front of Mel Dyson's long, split-level house. Brooks added his to the number. He and Jackie walked around to the back garden where they were greeted by Mel and his wife Kathy, Larry and Robin Sterling and three other couples, all gathered around a patio in a circle of lawn chairs. Nearby, several children kept busy playing badminton and flinging a Frisbee around. Mel had a portable bar on the patio, along with a cooler full of bottled beer and ice. He poured drinks for Brooks and Jackie.

'I like your house,' Jackie said.

'Oh, that's right,' Kathy exclaimed. 'This is your first time here. Come on, I'll give you the quick tour.'

Inside, she led Jackie from room to room, talking of wallpaper, tiles, panelling, furniture and the like. Jackie listened politely and made approving noises.

'Lovely,' Jackie said as they went back outside. She saw Brooks standing by the barbecue pit, talking, glass in hand, with Mel, who was listening attentively as he poked at the food with a long-handled fork. Hot dogs, hamburgers, steaks, ribs and chicken sizzled over the charcoal fire. Jackie took a seat next to the Sterlings. Robin was in the middle of a conversation, but Larry, less than engrossed by this subject, turned to Jackie with a smile.

'How's Mrs Matthews?' he asked pleasantly.

'Fine.' She liked Larry Sterling. He was a short man with dark curly hair and an expanding waistline, and he always seemed to be smiling, as if nothing could ever upset him completely.

'I'm glad to see Brooks come along,' Larry said.

'So am I. He's been working so hard lately.'

'I know. We've been getting it at the office, I can tell you.'

'Is it all just to do with this murderer? He seems to be so caught up in the case.'

Larry reached across to the cooler for another beer.

He twisted the cap off and peered at it for a second before answering. 'Well, it is a pretty important thing. Since this last killing, we've had the New York crowd in town, television, the press. Trying to make up their minds whether this is really a big deal or not.' Larry smirked.

'But Brooks—'

'Oh, he's awfully worked up about it,' Larry agreed. 'But that's the kind of man Brooks is. Once he starts something, he goes all out and doesn't let up until he's seen it through to the end.'

Jackie nodded. He might just as well have been describing the way Brooks had courted her from October to January.

'Most people aren't quite so strong-willed and persevering,' Larry continued. 'They're a little easier on themselves, but Brooks isn't made that way. And, so, there are times when it's a bit harder on those around him. But you wouldn't want him to change, would you?'

'No . . . no, of course not.' She knew Larry was right. 'I just . . . worry, I guess.'

'Wives always worry and the sun always comes up each morning.'

Now Mel was dishing out food enthusiastically, piling each plate high, all the while giving forth a kind of running pep-talk.

'There's a beautiful steak . . . Try the ribs, I made my own sauce . . . Those are good hot dogs, they contain no preservatives . . . Come on, Robin, you eat like a bird . . . Who made the salad? The radishes sure set your mouth on fire . . . Come on, Billy, eat the chicken leg, don't conduct an orchestra with it . . . How about you, Larry? Ready for more?'

After everyone had eaten their fill and resisted Mel's last attempts to force more food down their throats, Jackie gave Kathy a hand clearing up the paper plates and other rubbish.

When Jackie finished in the kitchen and returned to

the patio with a fresh drink, she saw that the men had wandered off across the lawn to pass judgement on Mel's vegetable patch. She sat down with the other women and listened to their conversation. Robin Sterling, a friendly but voluble redhead, was in charge again.

'Of course everybody knows there are drugs in the schools, even the grammar schools, why there isn't a school system in the country that's free of drug dealing, but all you can do is pray to God that *your* kids don't do something foolish—and if they do, that they don't get hurt or in any kind of trouble . . .' Robin paused only to catch her breath before continuing. 'Did you read that article in the *Star* the other day about . . .'

Jackie couldn't get too excited about this. It occurred to her that Brooks hadn't said two words to her since they arrived. He had spent virtually all of the time talking quietly with the other men. Work, she was sure. Mel and Larry and the others might or might not like it, but they certainly wouldn't quibble with Brooks. Somebody should, and Jackie knew it would have to be her, if anyone. They had to clear the air tonight.

She was simply not in the mood for idle chatter, so Jackie rose and left the other wives on the patio. She joined the kids playing with the Frisbee for a while. In the far corner of the lot, the husbands had settled around a redwood picnic table under a tree. Beer cans glinted in the late-afternoon sunlight. Blue smoke swirled up and then disappeared in the breeze. How ridiculous, Jackie thought. The men and women separated by the entire expanse of the back lawn, about as far apart as they could get and still be attending the same barbecue. Jackie drifted away from the Frisbee game.

Brooks was tapping the picnic table with his finger to emphasize some point when his wife approached. 'Hi, honey,' he said casually. 'What's up?'

Jackie came and stood beside him, placing one hand on his shoulder. 'Nothing, I just thought I'd see what the conference was all about.'

The men chuckled.

'Nothing much, just batting the breeze.'

'Politics, I bet,' Jackie said.

Brooks's face re-arranged itself unhappily and he shifted slightly on the bench.

'What it really is, Jackie,' Mel Dyson said as if he was letting her in on a big secret, 'is that we like being in the shade under this tree.' He grinned.

'The patio's in the shade too,' Jackie observed.

'Ah,' Mel exclaimed. 'But we like *this* shade.' Then he laughed, to prove that he had made a joke.

'Oh. Well . . .' Jackie began to feel that they regarded her as a child. No, not just her; all the wives. Whatever, she was now sorry she had intruded on this clubby gathering and she wanted to exit gracefully.

The oldest man there, an important-looking codger whose name Jackie could not recall, had been eyeing her up and down quite openly. Now he delivered his verdict.

'Handsome woman you got there, Brooks, handsome woman. Next time bring back one for me.'

Brooks smiled and the others laughed. Fortunately, Jackie didn't have to react to this. At that moment the Frisbee sailed to the ground a few feet away. She snatched it up and trotted away to return it to the kids. Christ, she thought, what a bunch they are together. Jackie was unsure whether to be angry over the way the men had treated her or dismiss it out of hand. No, she wouldn't mention it, she decided. She had more important things to talk to Brooks about. Jackie went back to the patio, where the subject of conversation seemed to be Bo Derek or statutory rape, or both.

'The husbands are having one of their private bull sessions, I see,' Kathy said with a sympathetic smile, bringing Jackie a fresh drink.

'Right.'

'They make it look serious but I think all they do is tell dirty jokes.' Kathy chuckled.

'I believe you.'

By the time the sun was setting Jackie felt tired and generally let down. The barbecue hadn't been as enjoyable as she had hoped and it certainly hadn't taken Brooks's mind off work—as far as she could tell. But driving home in the dark, Brooks loosened up and chatted freely with Jackie. He managed to smooth over that awkward moment at the picnic table, too.

'Bud's a funny old boy,' Brooks explained. 'He must be pushing seventy-five and he's still in practice —not much, but he keeps his hand in. And he's one of the canniest lawyers in the state of Utah. I hope he didn't bother you. These last few years he's been trying to turn himself into Salt Lake's Most Colourful Character, I guess. I've heard some funny stories about him . . . But he's a good man to know.'

He's saving the day, literally, Jackie thought as Brooks talked on. His face was expressive, fascinating to watch in the pale, coloured light from the dashboard. She found herself listening as much to the sound of his voice as to what he was saying, an experience familiar from their best moments together, and she knew again how much she was in love with this man. If only they could stay like this for ever, the two of them alone driving through the night, everything else a million miles away and gone . . .

But Jackie wasn't really sorry when they arrived home a few minutes later. She went into the house first, while Brooks put the car in the garage and locked up. Jackie left her bag and sunglasses on the kitchen table and went immediately to the study. There she turned on only the small green-shaded library lamp on Brooks's desk, then she stood in the shadows by the far window. Outside, she could see, fireflies moved randomly through the air, visible only when their eerie signals punctuated the dark.

'Oh, there you are,' Brooks said, entering the room. 'What are you doing here?'

'Waiting for you.'

'Yeah.' He dumped his keys, wallet and loose change on the desk, sat down and shuffled through some documents. He looked like he was merely sorting a few things into batches rather than settling down to do serious work. 'Well?'

'Hey.'

'What?' Brooks glanced over his shoulder at her.

'I can't talk to you when you're sitting at your desk with your back turned to me.'

Brooks seemed to consider this for a moment and then stood up and crossed the room to her. He took her chin in his hand. 'Okay, what is it?'

'Brooks.' She threw her arms around him. 'Hold me.'

He embraced her and kissed the top of her head. Then his strong arms lifted her off the ground against him until their faces were level and touching.

'Tell me,' he said softly.

Jackie didn't know whether to laugh or cry. 'Do you know how long it's been since we last made love?'

Brooks blinked.

'Too long,' Jackie answered her own question.

'I'm sorry—you know what it's been like for me.'

'You can't live like that, Brooks. Not all the time.'

'It'll be over soon, honey.'

'It's no good for either of us. I love you. I need you.'

Brooks set her down on her feet again. He gently brushed her hair back away from her face, and kissed her.

'Mmmmmmn . . .'

'Let's go,' he whispered.

'Where?'

'Upstairs.'

'Too far . . .' Jackie made sure the study was never quite the same room again.

ELEVEN
◆

Jackie felt better about things for a while. True, Brooks was still quite busy and he devoted little time or attention to his wife. But if nothing else, Jackie felt she had at least tried to help clear the air between them, and that gave her some temporary peace of mind. If married life was going to be more difficult than she had expected, she was not going to stand by without doing or saying something.

For a few days Jackie considered taking summer courses, but at the last minute she decided not to enrol. It seemed like more trouble than it was worth. You don't really care about getting a degree any more, she told herself. Besides, she knew how unpleasant it would be to have to study, how hard just to crack open a book, during the long, steamy summer months.

Jackie was glad she hadn't signed up for the courses when the telephone call came. It was Sandy, saying that she would be able to come out for a visit. Jackie was at the airport to meet her when she arrived in mid-July. They screamed happily when they first caught sight of each other in the terminal, jumped up and down hugging and kissing, and talked non-stop for hours.

'It's a fantastic place,' Sandy enthused as they sat down on the porch with a couple of tall, cool drinks. 'Just beautiful.'

'I love it,' Jackie said.

'You're looking good, you really are. But since when did you start smoking?'

Jackie tapped the cigarette in the ashtray self-consciously. 'I don't much. Just one now and then.'

That night Brooks took them out to dinner and he was more charming and outgoing than Jackie had seen him in many weeks. They had a marvellous evening together and at the end of it, when they were alone in their bedroom, Brooks grabbed the night-gown Jackie had been about to put on.

'You don't need that,' he said, tossing the flimsy garment aside. He took her in his arms and walked her, backwards, to the bed. *Yes, yes, this is my man.*

For the whole first week of Sandy's visit Brooks returned to something like what Jackie regarded as normal life. He came home a little earlier in the evenings and spent less time in his study. Jackie was pleased but she didn't know what to make of the change in him. Was it just because Sandy was here that he was making a special effort?

Brooks had planned to take the second week of Sandy's visit off from work so that the three of them could spend it at the cottage on Flaming Gorge Lake. But at the last minute he couldn't make it.

'We'll stay here until you're ready then,' Jackie said.

'No, you go on ahead. I'll follow you up as soon as I can get away. You can get your girl-talk finished so you can pay attention when I show you how to run a boat.'

'Why don't we just move the whole trip to next week?' Sandy suggested.

'I can't,' Brooks said. 'We've got another hearing scheduled then. With this investigation taking so much of our time, all of our other work is starting to pile up.'

'Are you sure you'll be able to get away? You won't end up being stuck here all week?' Jackie asked anxiously.

'Don't worry, I'll get away. I'll be up with you by Wednesday night, no matter what.'

'Do you solemnly swear?'

'I do,' Brooks said, laughing.

Jackie was disappointed but she let the matter stand at that point without further comment or question. As long as he got his damn business over and was at the lake by Wednesday night . . .

Late Sunday morning the car was packed with food and clothes, and the girls were ready to leave. Brooks stood by the front door of the house, waving. The powder-blue T-bird rolled down the drive, backed on to the road and started forward. Jackie tooted the horn once. They were away.

'You've been to the cottage before,' Sandy said.

'Once, back in April. Brooks and I opened the place up and aired it out after the long winter months, but it was still too cold for swimming.'

'Is it, you know, like, safe for us to be there on our own?'

Jackie laughed. 'Of course it is.'

'Let me see,' Sandy said, unfolding a road map. 'Now where are we going—Christ, it's a big lake.'

'Okay, do you see a place called Manila?'

'Manila . . . Okay, got it.'

'Follow the state line from there to the lake, and that's about where the cottage is.'

'It's out in the middle of nowhere,' Sandy said. 'What do you do in a place like that if you break your leg, with no telephone?'

'Mr Jenkins lives there, within eyesight and shouting distance. He's the fish and game warden. He has a wife and four kids, and they're very nice people, so you don't have to worry about a thing.'

The drive took a little over three hours, but it didn't seem so long as the girls kept up a lively chat and the scenery was spectacular.

'Last stop for beer and buckshot,' Jackie announced as they passed through Manila.

'Quite a metropolis,' Sandy said doubtfully. 'What do they do in the winter—hibernate?'

A short while later Jackie turned on to a dirt road through the woods. They continued for a few miles, and then came clear of the trees. The lake was alive with colour, rippling, almost dancing in the brilliant sun.

'God, it is beautiful,' Sandy said, trying to take in everything at once.

The dirt road wound through tall grass and into another clutch of trees. Five minutes later they came out on the other side and the cottage was right there, small but cosy-looking. Brooks had never painted the place, so the wood shingles were weathering slowly, naturally, from nutbrown to grey. Jackie turned the car in and parked alongside the cottage.

'Oh, I love it,' Sandy exclaimed. 'I just love it, what a setting!'

Steep, wooded hills and rocky rises loomed up behind them, less than a hundred yards away. On the other side the land sloped gently down to the lakefront. A rickety wooden pier reached a little way out into the water. Next to it was the long, low shed which served as a boathouse.

'That's the Jenkins house,' Jackie said, pointing to a large log cabin not quite a quarter of a mile further along the dirt road.

'That'd be some shout,' Sandy observed. 'I thought there would be lots of cottages here.'

'No, these are the only two places on this stretch of the lake. I think there are more, further up, into Wyoming, but we're the end of it here. And the other way, south, there isn't much usable frontage from here to the dam, miles away.'

They unloaded the car and settled in. Sandy was pleased to find that the cottage had hot and cold running water, a shower and toilet (Brooks had had a well drilled and a pump installed) as well as electricity.

'But no telephone and no television,' Jackie reminded her.

The ground floor consisted of a small kitchen, the bathroom and one large combined living- and dining-room. Upstairs were two bedrooms tucked under the sloping roof.

'Mind if I share your bed until Brooks gets here?' Sandy asked. 'If something comes crawling down from the hills late at night, I think we should face it together.'

'If you want,' Jackie replied, laughing. 'But it wouldn't be anything worse than a bear.'

'Oh, just a bear. And to think I was worried.' Sandy did put her suitcase in Jackie's room.

By the time they strolled along the lake-shore, visited the Jenkins family for a few minutes and walked back to the cottage, Jackie and Sandy were beginning to feel tired and hungry. Jackie had done the driving, so Sandy insisted on cooking. When they had finished and washed up, Jackie made a pitcher of martinis and they sat down on the back steps, facing the lake. A pleasure boat appeared far out on the water, circled and headed back the way it had come. Otherwise, the only sounds were made by birds, crickets and the easy lapping of the water. It was a supremely peaceful evening.

'I do like it,' Sandy said. 'The ideal place for a man and a woman to spend a lot of time chasing each other up and down the stairs.'

'Yeah,' wistfully. If only, Jackie thought.

'I still find it all hard to believe.'

'What?'

'How well you're doing,' Sandy said. 'A year ago you were just another student, like me, plodding along the well-worn path. Now you've got a terrific husband, a terrific house, a snazzy T-bird, and a summer cottage with a gorgeous lake thrown in for good measure.'

I wish it were what it looked like, Jackie thought, I wish it were as it should be . . .

'Come on,' Sandy said. 'You can tell me your secret now: how the hell did you do it?'

'I don't know. It just—happened. So fast.'

'That's love, I guess,' Sandy said with a theatrical sigh.

'I guess.'

'One thing about this place, though. I don't think you'll ever get your aunt out here.'

Jackie shook her head. 'No, I won't. In fact, I'm not sure I'll ever get her to Utah at all.'

'Oh, why?'

'I don't know, really. She refuses to fly, and I can't persuade her to take a train. Maybe she doesn't like the idea of making the long journey alone. I should visit her soon, and then I can try to get her to come with me when I return.'

'How is she?' Sandy asked. 'Is her health holding up?'

'Yes, she sounds all right. I talk to her every week.'

'That's good. Hey, you know you have mosquitoes here. Let's go inside.'

The next day they went swimming, hiked through the hills for a couple of hours, swam again and spent the rest of the afternoon lying in the sun. That evening it grew dark early and the wind coming in off the lake was gusty, racing through the trees noisily. A big storm is on the way, Jackie thought, and she was right. At first the lightning came in diffuse flashes, followed by a low rumbling of distant thunder. But soon it was on them in full force. The rain was driven down in great sheets, drumming the cottage furiously. Lightning lanced the sky in immense jagged arcs, bluish-white and purple chains that tore open the darkness. Thunder erupted in a staccato series of devastating, ear-numbing explosions that seemed to be going off all around the cottage. Jackie and Sandy, awed, a little frightened by the enormity of the forces at work, watched the storm through the screen door.

'I'm going out,' Jackie shouted suddenly.

'You're crazy.'

But Jackie was already outside and down the steps. Sandy stood in the doorway, waving and shouting to no avail.

Jackie was walking in the heart of the storm. The rain was falling so hard that it stung her flesh and made it difficult for her to see. She could hear the drops splatting loudly on her body. Her clothes were drenched in no time and her hair was smeared to her head and face. The thunder boomed and shrieked, seeming to buffet Jackie where she stood. Half-blinded by rain, and lightning so close she could smell the ozone, Jackie stopped and held her arms out. She had never witnessed a storm of such immeasurable power before. It was terrifying but also exciting to stand in the middle of it.

Sandy watched anxiously from the cottage. She wanted to get a drink but couldn't turn away. All was blackness out there, but for the sporadic, skeletal lightning. Each time it came she caught sight of Jackie again, a still figure in an instant of ghostly illumination.

TWELVE

◆

There are people who experience a strange sensation just before something important is going to happen. In a roadside café in the town of Manila, the young man felt a little shiver of excitement. It was brief and unexpected. All he was doing was sitting by the front window, dawdling over a second glass of iced tea. He turned and looked at the street outside. Quiet, nothing happening. This place was really nowhere. Then a shiny Thunderbird came along and drove past, with two girls in the front seat. Mmmn-hmmn. Nice, he thought. Funny how you can tell out-of-town when you see it, even when you're from out of town too.

He thought about the Thunderbird for a while. That is, a picture of it rolling by repeated itself in his mind several times. He didn't really get a good look at the girls inside the car, but that was just as well. If he had seen them, and they were ugly, what would he have to daydream about? Two girls in a T-bird . . . just think about it. He could have jumped in his own car and followed them—that would be easy out here—but something told him it wasn't necessary. So he didn't move, even though he felt as if he were missing something important.

'Getting kind of low,' the waitress said, examining his glass. 'Want another?'

'Yes, ma'am,' the young man replied, looking up with a quick smile. 'That'd be nice.'

He watched her as she went behind the counter, poured a fresh drink and brought it to him. Pretty good body still, he noted, but her face was just beginning to tell.

'There you are,' the waitress said, setting down the glass of iced tea in front of him.

'Thanks a lot. Good stuff on a day like this.'

The lunch crowd, if you could call it a crowd, had eaten and gone. The café was quiet now, so the waitress lingered for a moment, wiping the tabletop and straightening out the condiment tray.

'So what are you doing out here?' she asked. 'Just passing through, like everybody else?'

'Oh, I'm fishin' around,' the young man said. 'Thought I'd try my luck over at Flamin' Gorge. You know if it's any good?'

'I couldn't tell you. I'm not much up on fish.'

'Well, I might try anyhow.'

'Good luck.'

'Say, you look kinda tired.'

'It shows, huh?'

'No, I didn't mean it like, uh—to sound bad, you know.' He looked sheepish. 'I was just guessing and, maybe you do look a little tired around the eyes.'

'Yeah?' The waitress suppressed a smile. 'And . . . ?'

'I just meant, have you been on long today?'

She nodded. 'Since six this morning.'

'This place opens that early?'

'Sure.'

'Well, you must be getting off for the day pretty soon, right?'

The waitress shrugged noncommittally.

'Is that your name—Arlene?' He pointed a finger at

the gold stitching on her uniform. A good excuse to stare at her left tit for a second, he thought.

'Yes, this is my own personalized outfit,' Arlene said, but with only light sarcasm in her tone.

'Nice,' he said. 'So what time do you get off?'

'Get off?' she repeated with amusement. This kid really is an innocent. 'Why?'

'I don't know. Is there a good bar in town?'

'There's a bar. Why?'

'I just thought maybe we could have a drink and . . .'

'Oh yeah? What kind of fishing are you doing?'

He flashed his sheepish smile again. 'Well, if you had a few minutes you could tell me about this place. I have to find a—'

Arlene laughed. 'I don't need a few minutes to do that. What you see is what there is, and that's all.'

'All the same, uh . . .'

He was doing such a bad job of it that Arlene was almost tempted to help him out. In the year and a half she had been working at the café she had heard all sorts of lines from all sorts of men—cowboys, truckers, farm hands, junior hot-rodders and old-timers. Most of them weren't really on the make, but liked to compete with each other, and her, to see who could come up with the best sexual innuendo of the day. Some, of course, were serious, but Arlene knew how to fend them off without bruising their egos. However, this fellow seemed serious but rather naive. He was a grown man, but he still looked like a boy in some ways. If he was trying to pick her up, he sure didn't seem very practised in the art. He was not the usual amorous smoothie that came along from time to time. He needs lessons more than anything else, she decided.

'To answer your question,' she said, 'I get off when I'm finished.'

It was less than a come-hither look she gave him as she walked away, but it was more than just a smile.

Arlene went behind the counter and began cleaning up. The young man took another sip of iced tea and sat for a moment. Then he put some money on the table and left.

Down the street he found a package store, where he bought three bottles of sparkling white wine and a sack of ice cubes. He put them in a chest in the trunk of his car. *What nerve, what nerve, oh the chances we take. If the towns get any smaller we'll need a shoehorn to get in and out of 'em, right? We should of followed that T-bird, man. No? All right, all right . . . Later . . . I hear, I hear.*

He waited less than an hour before Arlene emerged from the diner. He fell in step just behind her, and then caught up. At first she was surprised to see him again, but then she chuckled.

'How about that drink now?'

'You mean it, you really do.'

'Sure I do. What do you say?'

She shook her head. 'Some other time, maybe. It's too early in the day for me. Thanks all the same.'

'Aw, come on. Lots of folks have a drink at lunch, and it's way past lunch now.'

Arlene laughed. 'Bring me back a nice Dolly Varden and we'll take it from there.'

Dolly Varden? 'Who the hell is she?' he asked.

'You're supposed to be the fisherman.' Arlene got into a VW convertible and started the engine. She looked back at the young man. 'See you,' she said with a wink. She put the car in gear and drove away, leaving him standing on the kerb.

'Son of a bitch,' he muttered.

Sometimes it's harder than other times. You screwed up, but tomorrow, tomorrow . . .

He bought a case of Coors and drove, popping one can of beer after another. Almost forty miles down the road, he pulled into a motel. The room was a sweatbox, the air conditioner sounded like someone dying of emphysema. He worked on the beer.

It's not over, but if you tell them they'll laugh and call you crazy. Is that what you want?

He slept until noon, showered and had something to eat before taking a leisurely drive back to Manila. Arlene came out of the diner at the same hour she had the day before. This time he watched her from a distance. She went to the post office, picked up some things at a grocery store, and then left town in her car. He stayed well back, but always kept her just in sight. A few miles outside of Manila, she turned on to a dirt road, heading up into the hills. Here he let her disappear from view, on the assumption that it was not a through-road and that it would have few if any turn-offs.

He drove slowly, studying the land as he went. It was wooded, but not heavily so. There were a few, widely scattered houses set back from the road along the way. At one point he spotted a small body of water through the trees at the foot of a long slope, and that made him smile. The road kept going. He began to wonder if he hadn't made a mistake after all. Maybe this did connect with a paved road somewhere up ahead. If it did, she was lost for another day—and then what would he do? He couldn't hang around a one-horse town like this indefinitely; he had taken too many risks already.

At the top of the hill he saw that the road ended about a hundred yards away. He also noticed the log cabin and the VW convertible parked beside it. Nice, he thought, a quiet retreat on a secluded hilltop in the middle of *fuckin' nowhere*. He drove to the end of the road, turned around and stopped the car. As he came up the path towards the cabin he saw a sandbox and a swing set out back. Kids? A husband? Hello, goodbye.

'What the hell are you doing here?' Arlene stepped out of the cabin and stood on the front step, her arms folded.

'Hey, hi there.' He stopped and wiped sweat from his forehead. 'I was fishing down below when I saw your car go by, so I thought I'd just say howdy.'

'There aren't any fish in that place. It's an old quarry.' She was cool and wary. No one had ever actually followed her all the way home before, and now, suddenly, here was this stranger standing on her ground.

'Is that a quarry? God damn, I thought it looked something like that. Those boys at the gas station sure must be havin' a laugh on me.'

'Yeah. Well. There's fish at Flaming Gorge.'

'Yeah, I'll have to try it. Too darn hot now, though. The rest of this day's shot.'

Arlene was studying him carefully. 'I don't have any iced tea,' she said. It wasn't hostile, but neither was it inviting. 'The neighbours should be by with my son in a few minutes.'

He smiled. It was easy to tell from the way she acted that she was alone here.

'Hey, that reminds me,' he said. 'I got something better.' He ran back to the car and fetched a bottle of sparkling wine from the chest in the trunk. The ice had melted but the bottles hadn't completely warmed up yet. 'How's this?'

Arlene laughed when she saw the wine. 'You're a hoot, you know that,' she said. 'Wait right here.' She came back a minute later with two glasses and sat down on the step. She had decided not to be rude and chase him away, but at the same time she was not about to let him into her house.

He poured the wine and then sat down on the grass a few feet away from her. 'Nice place you have here, real nice.'

'My husband built it.' Then she added, with a trace of sarcasm, 'From a kit.'

'Oh yeah? Well, it looks good to me. Say, he won't get mad or anything—I mean, me stopping by like this. I wouldn't want to, you know, cause trouble or—'

'He left two years ago,' Arlene said. She felt more at

ease now. 'He wanted to live here because he thought it would be a good place to raise a family, raise vegetables and think about God.'

'Is that right? What happened?'

'Eventually he saw the light. He had to immerse himself in the great energy field and spiritual vibrations that can only be found in a densely populated place. So he moved to LA.'

The young man plucked a piece of tall grass and chewed on the stem. 'Excuse me for saying so, but he don't sound like a very responsible guy to me.'

'He was a jerk,' Arlene said. 'And so was I. But at least I got this place out of it. I keep thinking I ought to sell it and pack up—but why should I? I've gotten kind of used to it now, and how do I know I'll like it any better somewhere else?'

'Hey, you're set up pretty good here.'

'It could be worse.'

'Yeah.'

They drank and talked for the rest of the afternoon. Arlene almost couldn't stop laughing when she saw him produce the other two bottles of sparkling wine. Her nine-year-old son, Mark, arrived home at one point, having hiked up the hill alone. He went to his room to watch television.

'Kids are great,' the young man said. 'I wouldn't mind having some of my own.' He looked as if he really meant it.

'Why don't you?' Arlene asked.

'Aw, I don't stay anywhere long enough, but maybe one of these days . . . Like they say, who knows?'

'Right.'

'Hey, I'd better get going now.' He stayed where he was, sitting on the grass. 'Time's rollin' on.'

Too much drink . . . You're going to make a mess of it.

'You can eat with us,' Arlene said. 'It's only tuna salad, but since you brought the wine, I should at least feed you.'

'Oh, thanks a lot. That sure beats a trip to the café.'

They went into the kitchen. Arlene took some vegetables out of the refrigerator and two cans of tuna fish from the cabinet. She turned to the electric can-opener and was about to plug it in when he jabbed the point of the knife blade deeply into the place where her spine rooted into the brain at the bottom of the skull. She was out before she hit the floor.

'Got it right first shot, see?' He was mildly surprised himself, but he couldn't keep I-told-you-so out of his voice. He made sure she was dead, and then he cut her eyes out, dropping them down her cleavage.

The mess, the mess . . . The kid, the kid . . .

'Hey Mark, your mother wants you,' he called out.

The boy came downstairs and died.

Outside, the sky had grown dark and the air was still, but heavy. Was that a rumble of distant thunder he heard? A storm was coming, for sure. He would have to work fast to finish the job before the rain came.

Hours later and two hundred miles away, he stopped the car and rested his head on the steering-wheel. They'll never be found, not where I've hid them. Was that a mistake? Too much, it's getting to be too much. No more zap, zap in the dark; each one has to be worked harder than the last. The chances we take. And now these two will never be found, so no one will know. It's a waste.

No it's not. There are bodies buried all over the place, these are just two more. And now, soon, soon . . .

THIRTEEN

♦

When the storm moved on Jackie finally went inside, feeling drained. It was as if she had been through some elemental rite she didn't entirely understand, an experience that left her dazed and limp. Sandy made her take a long, steaming hot shower, after which she forced Jackie to drink a whole pot of herbal tea. Bundled in robes and blankets, they played two sluggish games of cribbage and then went to bed. They slept holding each other for warmth.

The sun was back the next day, revealing the effects of the storm. The pier had tilted a little more, but otherwise survived. Many young trees had been swept over, bent nearly to the ground. A medium-sized oak had been shattered by lightning—only the torrential rain had prevented a dangerous fire. The dirt road had become a long stretch of mud, dotted with large pools of brown water. The lake was too cold to swim in.

The morning passed quietly and that afternoon Jackie and Sandy carefully navigated the car to the main road and drove into Manila for some wine. Bill and Ruth Jenkins had invited them to dinner that night. They stayed late and enjoyed themselves, getting back to the cottage just after one in the morning.

On Wednesday the lake was still rather cool, but by midday the land had dried sufficiently for Jackie and Sandy to go for another hike. They walked the high ground to the south, a terrain composed of mixed woods and rocky outcroppings. They made sure, always, to keep some tiny bit of the lake in sight. From one vantage point they could see great cloudy patches in the expanse of water below, which showed how unsettled the lake remained nearly forty-eight hours after the storm. Although everything seemed dry when they started out, Jackie and Sandy soon found that the shaded parts of the path they took were still quite soggy. Before long, their light sneakers were soiled and damp, their calves streaked with dirt, but they didn't mind.

'It amazes me that I'm actually here,' Sandy exclaimed. 'This is wilderness, hundreds of miles from anywhere.'

'You sound like I did a few months ago,' Jackie said, amused. 'It comes from spending the first twenty years of your life in towns and cities. You think of two trees together as vaguely menacing, and three constitute a definite threat.'

'I think it's great, but I suppose a person could get tired of all this nature from time to time. I mean, don't the Jenkinses ever get a sudden craving for a good Chinese meal?'

Jackie laughed. 'I don't know. Ask them.'

'Speaking of sudden cravings for exotic foods, are you going to get pregnant one of these days?'

'I don't know. I wouldn't mind.'

'I noticed you don't seem to be taking little whiteys any more.'

'No, I stopped. But nothing has happened.' Not much in bed either, Jackie thought sadly.

'Don't worry about it,' Sandy said. 'If you've been on the pill for any length of time and then stop, it takes your body system a while to adjust. Getting pregnant fast only occurs when you don't want it to happen; that's a law of science, or it should be.'

They paused for a short rest, sitting on a large flat rock in the sun, scraping mud from their shoes with sticks. When they resumed walking they hadn't gone very far before Jackie suddenly stopped.

'That's funny,' she said, bending over.

'What?'

'This, look.' Jackie cleared away the ground cover which partly obscured a crude stone tablet. 'I just noticed it when I stepped on it, my foot caught the edge. It must have been set upright originally but now it's almost completely on its back.'

'What is it, a marker of some kind? Thirty miles to beautiful downtown Manila?'

'A gravestone, more likely.' Jackie searched around, came up with a small rock and tried to chip away the crust of lichen and time which had grown over the curious object.

'A gravestone—here, in the middle of nowhere?'

'Sure, why not?' Jackie said. 'I bet it's been here for a hundred years or more.'

Ten minutes of laborious effort yielded very little. Jackie sat back on her heels and ran a finger along the three faint indentations which formed the letter Z.

'I think that's all you're going to get,' Sandy said.

'Z for Zeke.'

'Or Zachary. Or Zeb, Zebulon.'

'I have a feeling it's a Zeke,' Jackie said. She turned to look at Sandy. 'Do you realize that we must be the only two people in the world, in the whole world, who know he's buried here?' It made Jackie feel privileged to know that she had uncovered one of the planet's small, forgotten human secrets.

'Well, it might only have been somebody's dog,' Sandy remarked deflatingly. 'You never know.'

'It's a person,' Jackie said quietly, somehow certain that she was right. She took a last look at the roughly cut slab of stone and the solitary letter Z. Then they started the long trek back to the cottage.

Brooks hadn't arrived. In turn, Jackie and Sandy showered away the grime and sweat from their bodies, and washed their sneakers. Finally they ate, unable to put off supper any longer. By ten o'clock Jackie had lost all hope. In spite of his promise, Brooks would not be there. That evil seed which housed the twin black flowers of loneliness and despair took root in Jackie's heart and began to grow. She tried to bury herself in a book, but it didn't work. She had a very large martini, almost straight gin, and it managed to fuzz the edges somewhat, enabling her to find sleep a little more easily.

Late Thursday afternoon the youngest Jenkins child arrived at the door with a hastily written note, pencil lines that seemed to jerk and tremble on the beige paper.

> Jackie:
> Brooks just phoned to tell you that he's sorry he has been delayed. He hopes to get here tomorrow and he sends his love.
> *Ruth Jenkins*

But when the sun went down Friday night there was still no sign of Brooks. 'It's no big deal,' Sandy said soothingly. 'Imagine if he was a salesman on the road half the time, or an airline pilot zipping around the world with stewardesses to distract him. So Brooks couldn't get away after all—that's no reason for you to get so down.'

'He promised, Sandy.'

'And he meant it, but obviously something came up in the case he's on. That's not his fault, it's not anybody's fault. It's just one of those things that happen now and then. You think he's happy, stuck back there, having to work? Give the guy a break . . .'

Now and then, Jackie thought bitterly. Now and now and now and now, was more like it. And: Yes, I'm afraid he might be happy back there. Happy and in love—with his work. What really happened in that short, second marriage of his, had the woman found it impossible to cope with—*Oh, God, no, please, no, don't let me start to doubt him, us . . .*

Saturday, after swimming a little and lying in the sun, Jackie and Sandy decided to get good and drunk. They began drinking at four in the afternoon, large cocktails consisting mostly of mixers—'So we won't be unconscious in an hour,' Sandy declared. 'This is going to be an eight-hour Saturday-night campaign.' They skipped supper, or at least never got around to preparing it. A game of cribbage was started but eventually abandoned, as counting points became difficult and shuffling the deck a challenge in itself. Sandy was simply enjoying herself, but part of Jackie was driven, seeking to lose all thought and be overwhelmed by alcohol and the good feeling of being in the company of her closest friend.

It worked. At some point short of midnight, Jackie rose and, without saying another word, made her way deliberately up the stairs. She fell on to the bed and passed out. Sandy soon followed, just managing to pull the covers up over the both of them before her eyes closed and her mind went falling, spinning away.

Sandy awoke just before seven Sunday morning. Eyes all but shut, she stumbled and groped her way to the bathroom. When she returned to the bedroom she discovered, or, rather, now noticed that Jackie wasn't there. Sandy found her sitting cross-legged at the end of the pier. The morning was grey and a mist that would soon burn away in sunlight hung close to the surface of the lake.

'I feel like death warmed over—no, just death,' Sandy mumbled, seating herself beside Jackie. 'You don't look so good either.'

Jackie didn't speak. Her eyes remained fixed on some invisible point out in the middle of the lake.

'This is a silly place to be sitting,' Sandy said.

'There aren't two solid boards in the whole pier.'

'Brooks fishes from here,' Jackie said absently. 'He says he catches more here than he does out in the boat.'

'No fooling. Listen, can we—'

Jackie turned, and now Sandy could see that her friend's eyes were brimming with tears.

'Sandy—'

'Hey, are you—what is it, Jackie?'

Jackie put her face in her hands, trying to keep herself from giving way and sobbing uncontrollably. She felt Sandy's arm come around her shoulder, pulling her close. Her body was shaking and the tears streaked her face when she looked up.

'Sandy, I'm losing him.'

'Losing him? Brooks? What are you talking about, that's ridiculous.'

'I am, I know it.'

'Why? He can't have found some other woman, you've only been married—'

'No, not that, at least I don't think so.'

'What is it then? Tell me, Jackie.'

Slowly, painfully, it came out, bit by bit. His obsession with the murders, work, the endless hours he spent away from the house or shut in the study, the idle bed. Sandy listened patiently, willing her mind to concentrate in spite of the throbbing headache last night had bequeathed her.

'It's your fault,' she said gently but firmly when Jackie had finished.

'My fault? How?' Jackie wailed.

'You shouldn't have let it develop this way. You should have talked to him sooner, but you're still too much in awe of him and who he is—like when you first met. Jackie, he's your husband now, you can't be afraid to talk to him, to stand up and push when necessary. You can't just lie there and let whatever happens happen, hoping that somehow it'll be all right. Thank God it's not another woman, then you might really have trouble. But this is his job you're talking about, that's all. You can deal with that. He's a workaholic. You can beat that. But you've got to make the effort. He's had a long time alone, with nothing to occupy him but his work, so naturally it's become a way of life with him. He won't see his way clear unless you show him the way.' Sandy stopped, wondering if she had said too much . . . or too little.

Jackie sniffed and blinked back the last tears, breathing deeply to steady herself. She wanted to believe that Sandy was right, that she had been too diffident or deferential or submissive to Brooks's ways, and that the situation could be retrieved. But she had looked on this week at the lake as a kind of test. Brooks had not only not come, he hadn't even bothered himself beyond sending the briefest of messages and that by way of a third person. Something had opened up inside Jackie, a small but bottomless chasm of doubt. She didn't know if, much less how, it could be closed again.

The sun began to peek through, at once healing and merciless, scorching the mist which rose and twisted in the sudden glare, forming figures and shapes that swirled and danced on the surface of the lake before burning away completely.

FOURTEEN
◆

It finally happened, on one of those rare days when Jackie had been able to persuade Brooks to leave his office long enough to have some lunch with her. They went to an attractive café where they ate smoked salmon, dark bread and salad. Jackie drank two glasses of white wine while Brooks restricted himself to Perrier water. The conversation was pleasant enough, and unforced, but rather trivial. Still, it was better than nothing, Jackie told herself. She knew that a brief lunch with Brooks was hardly the time to bring up weighty matters.

The disappointment she had suffered as a result of Brooks's absence from the cottage at the lake forced Jackie to reconsider her attitude. If this was what marriage was going to be like, she would have to learn to snatch whatever good moments she could as they came along. Like Sandy said: the wives of ballplayers, pilots, salesmen and politicians can't expect to have the kind of archetypal family life you see on a television show. It ain't like that. Let me learn to adjust, Jackie wished silently over and over again; let me learn to be happy.

Brooks made his contribution to good cheer at lunch by mentioning the possibility of his going on another lecture tour in the autumn. He had a number of invitations from colleges and organizations on the West Coast. If he could find the time to work out the details and draw up an itinerary, and if he could be sure he could spare the time from the office in the autumn, well, then, perhaps they could hit the road. They? Brooks was determined to bring Jackie with him.

'Why don't you have your secretary arrange it all for you?' Jackie asked. 'Or I could do it.'

Brooks shook his head. 'The one time I let someone else make travel plans for me, the whole trip was a disaster,' he said. 'I'll take care of it, don't worry.'

Jackie smiled and acted pleased, but by now she knew better than to put much faith in Brooks's plans. To hope, to look forward to something, to expect —was to set yourself up for another letdown. When the time came, Brooks would probably scrap the lecture tour to stay home—and work. Or, if he did go, Jackie was sure that somehow, for one reason or another, she would be left behind.

What worried Jackie was the very real possibility that she would be unable to cope with this life for very long. Maybe not everyone is constitutionally built to make a marriage of sporadic, hit-and-run moments. A ballplayer's wife, after all, can at least count the days until the season ends and her man is hers again until next year. Jackie didn't even have that.

After lunch they walked back to the building where Brooks worked. He kissed her lightly on the cheek and they were about to part when Larry Sterling came rushing down the front steps.

'Brooks, they've got him,' he said, panting heavily.

'Damn,' Brooks exclaimed, as if angry with himself for having weakened and gone to lunch. 'Where is he?'

'They're bringing him in now, I was just on my way.'

'The Blade?' Jackie asked.

'Right.'

Brooks grabbed Jackie's hand, surprising her. 'Come on, honey. Let's take a look at this guy.'

She had to hurry to keep up with them as they strode down the street towards the police department two blocks away. But all Jackie was aware of was a great feeling of relief.

'Are they sure it's him?' Brooks demanded.

'Told me he was caught all but red-handed, that's all I know.'

'They've got the knife?'

'I guess so. Mercer down at the station, he's the one that phoned me, he sounded pleased as punch, like it was all wrapped up but good.'

'Where did they pick him up?'

'I don't even know that. I didn't stay on the line long enough to get any details—I told Mercer I'd be right over in person.'

Thank God, Jackie was thinking. Now maybe Brooks can slow down a little and get back to living some kind of personal life. And she wouldn't have to worry about becoming a nag.

Brooks leading, they went around to the rear entrance of the police building and down the long dark ramp used by the squad cars coming and going. A patrolman suddenly appeared, ready to stop them.

'Matthews, DA.'

Jackie had to suppress a giggle at the way Brooks had barked. It was like being in a cop show on television.

'Yes, sir,' the patrolman said quickly. 'I didn't recognize you at first.'

'Are they here yet?'

'Who?' The patrolman looked offended; he was on watch duty, pretty low shakes to be sure, but still, he should have been told if somebody special was expected.

Brooks steamed ahead without another word. This

better not be a false alarm, he thought. It could happen, oh, it certainly could happen. Especially when a police force is under pressure to come up with a killer. But at the bottom of the ramp things began to look promising. Around the corner, at the back desk entrance, there were maybe twenty blueshirts and about a half-dozen plainclothesmen standing around waiting. Brooks spotted a couple of local crime reporters as well, smiling and cheerful in the knowledge that they had the front-page story for today's late editions. Brooks and Larry plunged into the crowd, while Jackie stayed back to one side. Several policemen now engaged themselves in appraising her but she ignored them coolly. Then they all could hear the ugly sound of an approaching siren.

Although she too knew when the police car entered the long ramp, Jackie wasn't prepared for what was about to happen. The black-and-white swung sharply around the corner, past Jackie, and jerked to a halt at the door, one front tyre up on the kerb. The crowd, which had fallen back to make room, immediately surged forward again, engulfing the vehicle. The bank of red roof lights continued to flash sequentially, like a gambling machine signalling a pay-out, and the siren hadn't been turned off. Cameras flashed and clicked, and everyone seemed to start shouting at the same time. Jackie glanced through the plate glass window and saw Brooks and Larry standing with someone in the office—at least he wasn't part of this instant chaos.

The suspect was dragged out of the car. Jackie was surprised to see that he was a good-looking young man, and he was smiling in spite of what was going on. He wore faded, dusty denims, had light brown hair, and—that smile. So natural, pleasant, good-humoured. It was impossible to imagine this person hurting anyone, Jackie thought, but then she remembered that cliché about the most unlikely people always being the ones who turned out to be murderers.

But the young man's smile made things worse. He was dragged through the knot of policemen like a piece of baggage, even though he didn't show the slightest sign of resisting. Shouldn't the police be acting as guards and maintaining order? Jackie wondered. They were going about it in a strange way.

Shouts of abuse filled the air in competition with the siren. And then Jackie saw clenched fists zinging in, feet kicking out savagely. Finally the suspect was squeezed through the door into the office, and Jackie's last glimpse of him made her shudder. His left eye had been bruised and was already beginning to swell and blacken. Blood streamed from his nose. But he was still smiling.

The crowd continued to mill around for a while after the young man had disappeared from sight, but it thinned out. Like a scene from a western, Jackie thought, the angry mob . . . But these were policemen. Perhaps it was understandable, given the unusually hideous nature of the crimes and the fact that the victims were all young girls. But even so. Jackie found the whole thing disturbing, and she was sorry she had let Brooks drag her along. Come to think of it, why had he brought her here?

Larry Sterling came out of the office and walked over to Jackie.

'No point in you hanging around, Jackie,' he said. 'Brooks is going to be tied up inside, probably for the rest of the afternoon. Come on, I'll take you back to the street.'

They walked up the ramp.

'Why were they all trying to hit him?' she asked. 'He wasn't struggling with them.'

'Aagh—' Larry waved a hand dismissively. 'Some of those guys have to go home and tell their kids they slugged a killer.'

'That's terrible.'

'Well, some of them do feel very strongly.'

'Are they like that with all criminals?'

'Oh, no.' Larry's smile widened. 'They don't get nearly as worked up about shoplifters.'

They reached the street and stood in the bright sunshine.

'When will the trial be?' Jackie asked.

Larry laughed. 'A year, maybe two.'

'Really?' She didn't like the sound of that.

'If there's a trial at all,' Larry added.

'What do you mean?'

'The shrinks will get a crack at him, that's unavoidable, and it may end there if they decide he's a permanent mental case. Which wouldn't surprise me—did you see the way he was smiling?'

'Yes, I did.'

'Like he's just won a free trip to Disneyland. Anyhow, you know your way from here?'

'Sure, thanks, Larry.'

'Bye, Jackie, see you soon.'

She walked slowly back to the lot where her car was parked. Jackie saw now that she had been foolish to think the matter would end when the killer was arrested. It always took time for cases to come to trial, that was the way the system worked. Maybe they would get a quick confession, or maybe, as Larry said, the man would be locked up in a psychiatric hospital and never be heard of again. She hoped something like that would happen, that it could end quickly, because the idea that Brooks might be wrapped up in this case for another year or more was too disturbing for Jackie to think about at all.

On the way home that afternoon she was stopped for speeding. When he saw her licence and registration, and realized who she was, the state trooper put away his ticketbook and gave Jackie a verbal warning. She wouldn't remember a word of it, but something she said rang in her mind the rest of the way home.

Yes, that's right, I'm Mrs Brooks Matthews . . . Yes, that's right, I'm . . .

FIFTEEN
◆

August.

The one month of the year that can seem like a year in itself. The peak of summer heat and stillness. Roads soften. Lawns bake brown. The air grows thick and ripples with thermal currents. Hot dry winds blow down from the mountains. People move as if they were walking underwater. People sit motionless for hours in shaded rooms, but the sweat continues to pour from their bodies.

August.

A time of fruition. The gardens are full, the fields heavy. But plastics warp, forests burn and the air is like a fine warm powder in the throat of those who cannot escape. Children are beaten, hurled down stairs. People shoot their spouses. Or total strangers. Or themselves. People hang on their lives like forgotten laundry on a clothesline—empty and aimless, but there.

August.

Jackie at the airport, saying goodbye to Sandy. Stay, please stay—but the thought dies as soon as it is born. Whatever could have been said has been said, or lost

now. The impossible realities obtain. Their eyes lock in parting, and then Jackie is alone again. So alone.
August.
A shoebox café in Salt Lake City, across the street from the building in which Brooks works. Jackie sits staring out the window at that building. One cup of coffee, two, four. And the ashtray fills. Jackie sits. Staring.
August.
Brooks comes to bed very late again. Night after night. He lies naked on the sheet. Even at two-thirty in the morning it is hot. Jackie is awake. A whispered word, a touch—they do nothing. He is asleep in an instant, a man collapsed deeply into himself, gone again. Still as a dead man. A million miles away, on the same bed, the ache, the sense of loss. She feels his body rise and fall gently as he breathes. Is this all they have now, to be two people alive? Together. Alone.
August.
The pills that do no good. They get her to sleep, finally, but it is not a true sleep. She wakes feeling tired and groggy, a missing person struggling with the daylight world again. The pills keep her from dreaming, and she knows it. The dreams are necessary, perhaps now more than ever. But: another night, another pill. I'm doing it to myself, she thinks, but cannot stop. Night, oh night . . .
August.
The days begin, flowing like a vast river with slow, almost imperceptible currents, by afternoon becoming an endless sea with no horizon in any direction. This is the place that goes on for ever. Here you are not even drifting; you are becalmed. It does end, somehow, but then you find yourself ashore in the land of night again.
August.
Other wives. Telephone chats and visits over iced tea. But always, half an hour later, Jackie can't remember anything they spoke of. She is going through

the motions of . . . going through the motions . . .

August.

Jackie on the back lawn with a heavy shovel, trying to dig up clumps of grass. To dig a hole. To plant a tree she hasn't got yet. The sod is tough, thick with roots. Finally she gives up. She is grimy and drenched with sweat. The small scar on the expanse of green seems to mock her. In the distance, Rabar Penitentiary still stares at her. Even when she turns to walk away, she can feel it like a sore on the back of her head.

August.

Morning is not the worst time but by eleven it can already seem unbearable as the heat intensifies and the tidal pull to afternoon takes hold. Brooks was up early every morning and Jackie resisted the temptation to remain in bed, knowing that breakfast was one time when Brooks could be relied on to be cheerful and chatty—even if he was out the door and gone within ten or fifteen minutes. But today, as so often, Jackie was unable to steer the conversation to matters which she thought were important.

Jackie lit a cigarette as she heard Brooks drive away to work. She should get dressed, buy some groceries, have the T-bird washed (or wash it herself), pick some tomatoes and sweet corn from the garden, and occupy herself with a dozen other trivial chores. But she felt too tired today—no, not really tired but lifeless, devoid of the energy and desire to do anything at all. The sky looked like a vast sheet of zinc, largely grey, speckled with white. Like a lid clamping the heat to the ground, Jackie thought. She had taken two pills to get to sleep last night, it was so hot. Humid. Airless.

Jackie stubbed out her cigarette. She decided to go back to bed for a while, but first she went from room to room, pulling down the shades and drawing all the curtains closed on the ground floor. It might reduce the temperature inside the house by a few degrees, and even the slightest relief was welcome. She did the same thing upstairs, and then covered the bed with large fluffy towels. Jackie took off her robe and stepped into a heavenly cold shower for five minutes, after which, naked and soaking wet, she stretched out on the bed. Some of the water would be absorbed by the thick towels immediately, but the rest would cool her body as it evaporated.

Jackie lay on her back, watching the shades and curtains. Not the faintest hint of a breeze disturbed them. The only sound that came was that of an occasional car passing by on the road, a distant *rrhhmmm* that barely broke the quiet. Even the birds, usually so chirpy in the morning, were silent, as if they had finally come to their senses and decided to sit out the rest of this heat wave mutely.

Such a big bed, Jackie thought, and what a waste to use it only for sleeping. She looked down at herself on the bed—good breasts, a slim waist, nicely rounded but not large hips, long and slender legs. The body of an attractive, healthy twenty-one-year-old woman who kept herself trim and in shape. She put her hands to her face, as if expecting to discover, suddenly, some hideous scar, but she knew her complexion was blemish free. There's nothing wrong with me, Jackie told herself, and then wondered again why something was, nonetheless, wrong.

Perhaps it was because sex with her just wasn't good enough or interesting enough to Brooks, however much she might enjoy it. This point always brought Jackie close to a quicksand of insecurity and guilt: there's nothing wrong with him, therefore it must be my fault. She had slept with only two or three men before Brooks, but she reckoned she had learned a lot about sex with Todd Jackson, before things came to a jolting end. And dammit, *she knew*—she knew she was good in bed with Brooks. She knew from New York, from the country inns in Connecticut, from those hurried but exquisite sessions when the Parmenters left them alone at their house in Philadelphia, from the honeymoon and the first few months here in Utah—there could be no doubt, a person knew whether he or she satisfied the other person in bed.

It could be that she was building this matter up out of all proportion, that even as Brooks appeared to be obsessed with the Blade case she was letting sex become an obsession of her own. But the more time passed without it, the more she found it impossible not to think of it. The problem became greater by itself.

Jackie was dry now and she considered stepping into the cold shower again, but inertia made the decision for her and she remained on the bed. She let her eyes close and her mind drift free of thought. For a long time she lay there, passing into and out of sleep, changing her position slightly now and then.

She heard it first, without knowing what it was. Jackie lifted her head, trying to focus her attention. It was a soft, random tinkling sound. Then she realized it must be the crystal chandelier in the downstairs front hallway. A breeze at last? Jackie glanced at the windows, but the curtains hung forlornly in the heat, the shades moved not at all. This is the back of the house, Jackie reminded herself.

What time is it—how long have I been lying here? She looked at the clock-radio on the bedside table. Just after eleven—God, a couple of hours. The chandelier continued to chime itself. Jackie started to get up but then she stopped and looked at the clock again. Something strange was happening. The illuminated red digital clock face was flashing, now on, now off, dimming, flickering, the numbers 11:04 going black and disappearing only to relight again at full power, fade to a dull rosy glow, blank out and promptly resume its flash in a fit of crimson shuddering. Jackie tried to make sense of it but thought came slowly, she wasn't fully awake yet. She turned on the small table lamp, and it flickered in time with the clock. She switched it off, fumbled with her bathrobe and went downstairs.

It was the chandelier tinkling and chiming against itself, Jackie saw when she reached the hallway. It was swaying gently, as if in a breeze. But there was no breeze. She went to the door and put her face to the mesh screen. No breeze, not a whiff of movement in the dense, syrupy air. Jackie opened her mouth to breathe, gulping like a goldfish for oxygen.

She couldn't think. Her mind was like something all gummed up, reduced to fitful, inconclusive spasms of thought. It was the sleeping-pills, she knew. They seemed to have a cumulative effect, keeping her dopey a little longer each day. Jackie told herself she should try to fight against it, but then she wondered: Why? It helped to get her through the day. It wasn't unpleasant. In fact, it was even starting to feel rather comfortable. Like sleep-walking, but you were conscious and in control, more or less.

She found herself in the living-room. Daylight filtering through the shades filled the space with a dark, orange glow. Now, here, there was movement. A man was sitting on the floor, his back to a chair. As in a dream, Jackie felt alarm, uncertainty, amazement, but in a detached way, as if she was not only taking part in the scene but also observing it from some point outside herself. Unable to speak, she stood looking with wonder on the figure seated before her.

'Hi there,' he said in a genial tone. 'Hey, I hope you don't mind me sitting here and havin' a beer. It's a bitch of a day out there. Why don't you have one too?'

Jackie never drank beer, but hardly had he spoken the words when she was sitting on the carpet near him, putting a green bottle to her lips. The icy liquid felt good in her throat.

'Sure is nothin' like a frosty beer on a bitch of a day like this, I tell you.'

He was young, about her age. Dusty blond hair.

Two or three days' beard stubble. Dirty, faded denims. Cowboy boots, scuffed and cracking. A smell of outdoors, soil, leaves. Friendly eyes, a good face that was not handsome but easy to look at. Boyish grins. A relaxed, south-western country accent.

'I've been on the road so long, seems like that's all I do, first one place then another. Can't seem to settle in one spot for any length of time, y'know. Some folks say that's a helluva way to live, and I guess they're right, but when you've done something long enough you get to the point where you don't know any other way. I been like that all my life, don't suppose I'll change now.

'A house like this—you got it good here. This is the way everybody should live. But me? I'd start off okay in a house like this, but after a while I'd start to feelin' cooped up and then—zoom, there I go, down the road again. Don't know where I'm goin' or what I'm lookin' for, but I'm gone. You think that means I ain't grown up? Shit, I think some folks are just born that way.

'But that don't mean you don't learn nothin' or you can't make your way. One guy's good at carpentering and another guy, he's got the knack for working with cars. Somebody else is good at numbers and bullshit and so he makes fancy deals for himself. Me, I ain't ever learned those kinds of things, but I get along. That's what I'm good at, getting along. You learn all kinds of funny things, that's for sure.

'I'll give you an example. Food and water. You always got to have food and water. Most people, you take them out of their pretty homes and cute little towns, and drop them somewhere into the woods or the desert or the plains, and they'll be in trouble. 'Cause there ain't no Safeway out there selling food. They ain't learned how to take care of themselves. Me, I can find food and water anywhere, the desert, you name it. Hell, I've had to. I can find water where you'd never dream there was any, 'cause I've got a feel for the land and I know where to look. You've heard of Death Valley, the Badlands, the Sandhills of Oklahoma—I been through those places.

'And food, I can always get food. I'll tell you, once I was on the move, long way from any town and hungrier than hell, and I stopped by a little water hole. No fish, it was too small for fish, and not even one goddamn frog. But I remembered a trick some old boy once told me and I gave it a try. I danced around that hole, stomping my feet and singing loud as I could. If somebody'd come along then they'd've figured me for plain crazy. But sure enough, it worked. One dumb turtle had been sittin' down there in the muddy water and weeds, layin' low, and he had to come up to find out what all that racket was. Turtles are curious beasts, and dumb as rocks. I didn't know that turtle was down there, but I got 'm and had a nice dinner. Now, you go into the city and you'll find people that pay a lotta money for a little bowl of turtle soup, and those people wouldn't know which end of a turtle was front or back if it was all tucked in the shell.

'So, there's different ways of bein' smart, and I guess I get along as good as anybody else, all things considered. I don't worry—a lotta people worry, you know, but I don't. I know I can look after myself, and if the time comes when I can't, well, ever'body's gonna die anyway, sooner or later. Ain't much point in worryin' about it.

'But you gotta watch out for people, they'll really bitch you up if you let 'em. The thing is, they can't stand to leave each other alone, always got to start something. You don't look and act and be like they want, they start to get on your case and make life miserable for you. I hate that. And it's the same the higher up you go. Lord, I'm just trying to get along, waiting for that day which I know is comin' and is gonna change everything. They're gonna start chuckin' all those missiles and rockets and droppin' A-bombs . . . And it's gonna blow them all away and burn off all the shit like the fire of God.

'And I'm waitin' for that, because when that happens the only ones left are gonna be people like me, just a few who know how to take care of themselves. And money won't mean a damn thing any more. That day'll come, you can be sure of it.

'I'll tell you, though, what is hard about the way I live is women. I can't seem to settle in one place for very long and that makes it hard to get anything goin' with a woman, you know. Soon as I think I found one, bang, I'm sick of the job and headin' for the next town, where I gotta start all over again with some other woman, knowin' I'll probably leave again before too long. That kinda messes you up inside after a while. Being alone so much. I keep thinkin' I'll meet some gal like me, who likes to move around, but it ain't happened.

'Oh, a coupla times it looked like I got lucky, but then it never lasted long. They meet another guy and decide to drop anchor in some town when I'm ready to go, or they just get tired and babyish and run back home to Daddy. I don't know, I hate to hurt anyone but people seem to do it easy as fallin' off a log. Boy, that burns me.

'Here I am talkin' away and you haven't said a word, but I can tell that you know what I mean. Just lookin' at you I can see that you're a good person. You listen, you see and your eyes aren't hard. You care.'

He leaned forward and pulled open Jackie's bathrobe, exposing her breasts. She didn't—couldn't move.

'You're so young and beautiful. Meetin' a woman like you . . . But there's a sadness in you that shouldn't be. We all know it, we all have it in us, but most folks don't like to think about it. In fact, most people you meet have got so they don't even recognize it any more, they got it buried so deep. But it's still there, and you and I know what it is . . . Hunger . . . Aching . . . Loneliness . . .'

He stroked her breasts and his touch was like a jolt of electricity buzzing through her body. He clutched her hair and pulled her face to his. He was rough but not violent or hurtful. Jackie's mind, entranced from the moment she had walked into the room, gave up its last hold on awareness and spiralled away into the infinite sea of the senses as her eyes closed.

It was a dream—at last, a dream, again—and her mind was running free once more. But this time it was her body speaking, singing with passion. Spontaneous and elemental—like comets through her brain.

They moved together and every part of Jackie's body felt like it was exploding, every cell longing for the obliteration that pleasure brings, flaring with acceptance.

Jackie understood what was happening. She was disappearing, drowning joyously in the ocean that touches no shore. The ocean that now seemed so sweet. They would find welcome, and great peace, in each other. Words burned in her heart.

I've been waiting.
So long.
I need you.
Take me.
I don't want to be alone.
Take me and take me with you.

'I will,' he whispered, entering her.

3
♦
SHADOWS

SIXTEEN
◆

The screen door slammed.

Footsteps in the hallway.

Jackie jumped, startled and awake. She looked around and saw that she was on the bed, upstairs, naked. The clock showed 4:42. Jackie was confused and she tried to clear her thoughts. Was it all nothing more than a dream? Had she been lying here all this time, sleeping, caught up in a long erotic fantasy? Had she masturbated?

No, no, it was coming back to her now. It had been too real to be a dream. The sound of his voice, the feel of his touch, his lean, hard body—were still vivid in Jackie's mind. But then, in a way that was even worse. It meant that she had let a complete stranger walk into their house, help himself to beer from the fridge, get off with her on the floor and then leave. It was absurd, impossible. Humiliating. She wouldn't behave like that—would she? Jackie remembered that she hadn't even reacted to finding him in the livingroom; it was like she had been hypnotized, or drugged. It *was* like a dream, and yet her body told her it had been real.

Jackie heard a distant voice. Brooks, talking to someone on the telephone downstairs. God, that had been him coming in the front door just a minute ago. She yanked the towels from the bed, hurried to put them away and then pulled on some clothes. When she looked, she found no empty beer bottles in the living-room or kitchen.

'Hey, there you are,' Brooks said. He kissed her lightly on the cheek. 'Where were you?'

'Upstairs, resting.'

'You look terrible, honey.' Brooks took a carton from the refrigerator and poured a glass of milk. 'What did you do today?'

I wish I knew, Jackie thought. 'Nothing. Took cold showers and slept.'

'Are you all right?' Brooks asked with concern.

'Just the heat. I guess it got to me. I could hardly move, I felt so washed-out.'

'Is that why you pulled all the curtains and shades? This place is so dark it looks like the last act of *Mourning Becomes Electra.*'

Jackie managed a smile. 'I thought it would help cool the house a little.'

'That's a common misconception,' Brooks said. He finished the milk and poured another glassful. 'It actually impedes the flow of air and makes the heat worse.'

'Really? But there was no air, and if there was, it sure wasn't flowing.'

'Yes, I know what you mean. Maybe I'll put some air-conditioning in, now that I've got someone who'd use it during the day. Say, did you notice anything funny this morning? Maybe you were sleeping. Around eleven?'

'Like what?' Jackie asked, looking away.

'Well, if you had a light on it might have flickered and dimmed for a minute, or—'

'Yes, I happened to look at the clock-radio at 11:04 and it was behaving strangely.'

'Right, there you are,' Brooks said, smiling broadly. 'What was it?'

'I had a meeting with the warden at Rabar,' he explained. 'Now, all of Cleary Centre is on the same power grid as the prison and this morning they ran their annual inspection test on the electric chair. Strictly routine, but I guess they gave it too much juice. The utility boys were on the phone in a hurry, raising hell.' Brooks chuckled as he recalled the incident.

Testing the electric chair, Jackie thought. How morbid. To think that at the same time Brooks was observing that little ritual, she was . . .

'Brooks, can we sit down and talk for a few minutes?'

'You are feeling all right, honey?'

'Yes, better. I think we—'

'Good, because you're not forgetting that we have to go out this evening.'

'Out? Where?'

'The testimonial dinner for Wayne Hunter. I did tell you about it.'

'Oh, hell, yes.' Jackie sighed. Another one of those wretched functions to which Brooks was always being invited. Of course I have to go too, she thought miserably, I'm his wife after all, remember? Half of the men would try to impress her while the other half would ask her transparent questions and give her sly looks. As for the wives, well, they went with the men. Bores all.

'So we'd better start getting ready,' Brooks was saying. 'You'll have to do your hair and—'

'Yes, okay.'

Another missed opportunity. Or maybe it was simply another non-opportunity. Whatever they are, I get them, Jackie reflected bitterly. But she knew it was her own fault. If she had doubted Sandy's words at first, she had come to see that she was indeed failing to force things with Brooks. He was living his life. It was up to Jackie to establish her place in it, to develop her identity and role within the relationship and make sure he didn't neglect it. But she wasn't doing so. Instead, she was letting Brooks carry on, probably as he had been for the last twenty years. He had gone out and got himself a wife, and that seemed to be the end of it as far as he was concerned. Not good, but she was equally to blame for letting it happen.

She could have a long, serious talk with Brooks if she really wanted it. They lived together, it wasn't impossible. But she always stopped short and let the moment pass. When she and Sandy had returned from the cottage at Flaming Gorge Lake, Jackie had made it clear to Brooks how displeased she was that he hadn't joined them there. But he apologized profusely and Sandy forgave him quickly—too quickly for Jackie's liking—and Jackie was unable to do anything but let the matter drop.

What am I afraid of? Jackie wondered as she prepared for the testimonial. Afraid that she would seem like a whining, nagging child-wife? Afraid that she was being selfish when his work was obviously of considerable importance, not just to himself but to the entire community? Afraid that she wouldn't have a chance of matching up to him if it came to any kind of argument? Afraid, most of all, that he might say, This is the way it is, sometimes it's good and sometimes it's not so good, but that's the way my life is and we have to do the best we can with it? Afraid to say, What about *my* life . . .?

In the car as Brooks drove, he talked about The Blade case. He was pleased with the way it was shaping up. Not that it was as open-and-shut as he would like, but he had no doubt he could bring in the right verdict. Jack Tate, the suspect in custody, would have to take the stand and testify on his own behalf, otherwise he wouldn't have even the remotest of chances. Brooks was sure he understood how Tate worked, as a person, and he was convinced that Tate lacked the inner strength, that core of character and will and nerve to successfully portray himself as a harmless migrant worker, an innocent victim of a society's need to find and punish a wrongdoer.

When Tate took the stand and faced Brooks in court, it would become a matter of two personalities clashing, warring with each other. But Tate could not defend himself; he would be up against a man who, like a chess master, knew how to maintain the initiative and steadily increase the pressure. Brooks would systematically grind down Tate's ego and ultimately crush the man.

Listening to all of this only depressed Jackie. It sounded like some ghastly sport, the playing of which was its own justification. Truth and justice and all those other cornball notions were marginal. One more lesson in the education of an ex-student discovering real life, Jackie thought sadly.

If she became cynical about his work they would really be losing touch with each other in every way, she realized. Would politics be any different—how would she react to the inevitable wheeling and dealing? She was Mrs Matthews. Brooks's pretty bauble. That's it, admit it to yourself. A man in his position, with his ambitions—he needs a wife. Someone attractive and polite and—his. One more credential in the portfolio. The fact that she was so young—well, that had a certain curiosity value and added a drop of spice to the equation. Brooks knew what an asset a lovely young wife had been to John Kennedy, and now Brooks had an even younger Jackie of his own.

She shook her head, as if these thoughts could be dismissed physically. That way lies paranoia. Brooks was not that cold and calculating. But Jackie still had a feeling that she might be approaching some kind of corner, perhaps had already turned it. What had taken place that morning made a difference, one that would permanently affect the way she saw herself and Brooks.

That man, the mysterious young stranger who had appeared as in a dream, wielding almost godlike control over her, had touched her profoundly, irrevocably, reaching her heart and her mind and her body. It didn't matter whether he was real or a fantasy, and it wouldn't prevent her from fighting for her marriage, as she knew she must.

But if the stranger ever returned, she would welcome him gladly.

SEVENTEEN
◆

'Jack, you look like you don't have a worry in the world,' Lieutenant Mercer said at the start of the third interrogation.

Jack Tate had his feet on the desk and a big lazy smile on his face. 'Worryin' won't do me no good,' he said nonchalantly. 'Besides, I got witnesses.'

'They don't sound that positive to me, Jack. I would say you're far from being completely covered on all the dates and places. In fact, I'd go so far as to say that you're in deep, deep trouble.'

Tate's smile didn't waver. 'Well, you boys are gonna do whatever you have a mind to do with me. It's out of my hands now.'

'Why don't you make it easier on everybody, yourself included, by helping us out on this? What's the point of slowing it all up and dragging it out?'

'What do you want me to do—confess? I told you before, it wasn't me who killed those folks. Hell, I like girls, Lieutenant.'

'Especially young ones, high school girls?'

'Sure, but that don't mean I'd kill 'em.'

'What do you do to them, Jack?'

Suddenly Tate turned to the large mirror on the wall nearby. 'Hi folks,' he called out, waving a hand. 'How you doin' in there? Here comes the dirty part.'

On the other side of the one-way glass, in a small dark room, Brooks Matthews and five other people sat stolidly, observing the interrogation. Another man, a technician, was recording it on videotape.

'Half-assed wise guy,' Brooks whispered to Mel Dyson. 'They're the easiest ones to get.'

'Jack, do yourself a favour,' Lieutenant Mercer continued. 'Don't fart around. This is a serious matter; it could mean your life.'

'Aw, shit, well that's different. What do you want to know?'

'You were going to tell me what you do with young girls, high school girls, like Martha Raeburn.'

'Her I don't know,' Tate asserted. 'But as for other girls, well, I hug 'em and I squeeze 'em and they don't even know my name, 'cause I'm The Wanderer.'

'Is that what you call yourself?' Mercer asked seriously.

Tate laughed. 'That's from an old song, Lieutenant. I just wanted to see if you knew it.'

'I don't care if it's from an old song, Jack. I wonder if there isn't more to it than just that. Does the song have special meaning for you?'

'You guys really are desperate,' Tate declared with a pleased look on his face. 'I roam from town to town—that's in the song too. Just like my life, see? Go ahead, Lieutenant, make something of it.'

Tate's last remark sounded as if he were daring the police to waste time on an irrelevancy, but there was also a note of defiance in his voice. Mercer decided to drop the question of the song for a few minutes.

'Jack, the other day you told Detective Singer that you knew something about these killings.'

'If you say so, I guess I did.'

'What do you know?'

'What I've read in the papers, that's all.'

'Detective Singer had the impression from the way you said that to him, Jack, that you meant you know more about the killings than just what's in the newspapers. Do you?'

Tate shrugged. 'Like everybody else, I have my own thoughts on the subject and I've formed my own opinions. But that don't mean I have any hard facts or inside information.'

'Okay,' Mercer said reasonably. 'How about letting me know your thoughts and opinions? They might be of help to us.'

'I think you oughta look for a young guy, early twenties. Tall but not real tall, maybe six-one. Light hair, lean build. A drifter probably, no fixed address, no regular job. A guy with a mysterious past, maybe. That's what I think.'

Lieutenant Mercer stared at Tate.

'Someone like you.'

'That's right,' Tate agreed promptly. 'Someone *like* me.'

'Jack, you're ready-made for this rap.'

'Now we're gettin' down to cop-talk,' Tate said, turning to direct a wink at the mirror.

'You were caught with a girl in a secluded spot, with a knife in your hand,' Mercer said, sharpening his tone of voice.

'It was under the seat, I told you, where it always is. That cop was lying—he just wants to be the one who gets the credit.'

'What were you doing out there with that girl when you were caught?'

'Chasin' pussy, what the hell do you think?'

'With a knife?'

'You want to know what I think?' Tate asked. 'That proves it wasn't me who killed those girls.'

'Jesus Christ, how do you figure that one?'

'Easy,' Tate said with his confident smile. 'All those girls were killed outdoors or in some place that was familiar to them, like the one in her own house —right?'

'Go on.'

'I'm just goin' on what I've heard,' Tate added before continuing. 'So if I was the killer, why would I suddenly change methods and kill a girl *in my car?* There'd be blood all over the seats and carpet and —just think of the mess. No, your killer would never go about it that way.'

It was Mercer's turn to shrug. 'You won't get that one off the ground,' he told Tate. 'As far as we're concerned, you were going to use the knife first to force the girl out of the car, and then to finish her off.'

'That knife was under the seat,' Tate repeated stubbornly. 'It wasn't me who cut up those little girls.'

'Who was it, Jack?'

'I don't know.'

'Tell me some more of your thoughts and opinions then. Why would anybody want to do such vicious things to people who never did him any harm?'

In the next room Brooks turned again to Mel Dyson and said quietly, 'Mercer is a second-rater. He should keep the pressure on all the time, bam-bam-bam.'

'I know what you mean,' Dyson said. 'But he's never had to handle anything like this before.'

'It's going to be up to us to carry the ball on this one,' Matthews said.

'—the slightest idea,' Tate was answering the Lieutenant's question. 'Maybe he's gettin' back at something somebody did to him. Maybe he's just crazy in the head.'

'I think he must be a little sick to do things like that, don't you agree?'

Tate sat up abruptly. 'Hey, I just thought of something,' he said. 'If I confess and get convicted, can I collect the hundred-thousand-dollar reward that's been posted?'

'Don't be stupid,' the policeman said angrily.

'I just don't like the thought of that cop getting it, you know? That'd annoy the hell outta me.'

'Jack, you're setting yourself up for a mighty big fall if you don't co-operate with us on this. I'm telling you, and that's no joke.'

Tate leaned across the desk and for the first time he looked completely serious.

'Lieutenant, I was set up for a fall a long time ago. Now it's all too late. Everything that happens from here on out just happens on its own.'

'What do you mean?'

'A rock starts rollin' down the side of a mountain, it won't stop till it gets to the bottom.'

'What do you mean you were set up, Jack?'

'Aw fuck it.'

'No, tell me, Jack. Really. I'm here to listen and find out what the truth is. I can't help you if you don't help me.'

'Avalanche.'

'What's that supposed to mean?' Mercer asked patiently.

Behind the one-way glass Brooks muttered in exasperation, 'Bullshit. He's leading Mercer around in circles, treating him like a dog on a leash, for Chrissake.'

'I could tell you a lot of things,' Tate said to Mercer. 'Things I think of when I'm alone on the road. Things you'd never believe. But what's the point? It sure as hell doesn't matter any more.'

'It might matter a whole helluva lot,' Mercer said. 'Why don't you tell me more about it and we'll see if it means anything or not?'

Tate laughed with genuine amusement. 'Do you want to solve the case or do you want to arrive at the truth?'

'If we do one, we do the other,' the policeman declared. 'What's the difference?'

'Could be plenty. Could be all the difference in the

world, but I guess it don't matter now.'

Mercer sighed wearily. 'Jack, we've been talking all over and around this business, and yet we've been avoiding the heart of it. I've got a feeling that you do know something, and that you really do want to tell me, or somebody, about it. What do you say? Your neck is on the line and you got nowhere to turn now, Jack. I promise you, you'll feel a hundred per cent better inside if you'll just open up and get it all out.'

'Lieutenant.'

'What is it, Jack?'

'Do me a favour: stop calling me Jack. It's a cheap traffic-cop trick and I don't like it. You're not my friend.'

'I only want to get to the bottom of this. I'd like your help and I'd like to help you. But one way or another, I will get to the bottom of it.'

'You may solve the case, but there's a lot more to it than that. Things you'll never know or figure out.'

'Sure, Jack.' Mercer looked bored and he gathered up his notes. 'Let me know if you want to tell me about it some time.'

It almost worked. Tate sat up quickly. He liked these sessions and didn't want this one to end so soon.

'I'll tell you this,' he offered. 'There's more than one person involved. I'm sure of that.'

Mercer stood up but made no move to leave the room. 'How do you know that, Jack?'

'I'm telling you there's others involved in this,' Tate insisted. 'It's too much for one person, it's too much for me. I don't know all of it, or even a half of it, but—'

'Come on, Jack, we know it was the work of one man, a solitary, disturbed individual.'

'You think I'm disturbed?'

'Don't you?'

'I think you're all wrong, Lieutenant, that's what I think. In fact, I know it.'

'So long, Jack.' Mercer walked to the door.

'More than one, Lieutenant,' Tate called out. 'More than one, don't kid yourself.'

He turned to the mirror on the wall and bared his teeth in the kind of hideous death-grin of a naked skull.

EIGHTEEN

◆

The next few weeks seemed to bear out Jackie's worst fears. With a suspect in custody, Brooks became even more engrossed in the case. He sat in on several of the interrogations and made duplicate tapes of all the others, sitting up late at night in his study, playing them over and over. Slowly, painfully, he was building his case.

It wasn't easy. The man they held, Jack Tate, was an elusive character. He was born in Texas twenty-four years ago, had no criminal record and no family that he knew of now. The last six years, he claimed, he had spent drifting around the western states, doing farm work and odd jobs. Tate would admit to no involvement in the crimes he was suspected of having committed, but everyone who met him had the same general impression—he wasn't telling the truth, or at least not all of it all the time. Tate could be convincingly naïve or transparently sly, goading, helpful, dissembling, eager, shy or indifferent—ringing the changes from one moment to the next.

It was precisely this which persuaded Brooks that they did indeed have the right man. Tate talked to the police, he was always willing to talk to them, a fact which exasperated his court-appointed lawyer no end. To Brooks it meant that Tate had a great deal of self-confidence; more, a pretty large ego. The police, the District Attorney's office, the horrendous charges and the threat of the electric chair—all a game to Tate, who was happy to take on the challenge in his folksy way. His ego would undo him in the end, Brooks believed. With patience and attention, the way would become clear. But there was no doubt: they had the right man. As he sat back listening to Tate's lazy drawl roll off the tape, night after night, Brooks was sure he could put together the case and prosecute it successfully. It just had to be done right.

The one tangible piece of evidence they had was the knife. Tate had been captured while sitting in his car with a girl he had picked up only a few minutes earlier. They were parked on a dirt track off a country road just outside of Orem. A passing state trooper caught a glimpse of the car from the road, stopped and approached on foot. The trooper reported that Tate was kissing the girl and had the knife in his hand when he put the barrel of his service revolver to the back of Tate's head. Tate said he was kissing the girl and that the knife was where he always left it, under the driver's seat, nothing more sinister than that. Plenty of people had hunting-knives, they were perfectly legal. There were traces of human blood on the knife, but Tate and most of the dead girls shared the same common type. Still, it was something, and a jury would believe a state trooper over a transient most of the time.

While Brooks was busy trying to unravel Jack Tate his wife tried her best to be understanding and tolerant. But it wasn't easy. Since that night after Mel's barbecue, when they made love in the study, Jackie and Brooks had had sex exactly once more. He was out of the house early in the morning, only occasionally available for a quick bite of lunch, and sequestered in his study after dinner until late. Weekends were hardly any better; Saturday and Sunday were good days for Brooks to drive around the state, going from one town to another, interviewing potential witnesses. It didn't matter that these people had already been interrogated, Brooks had to ask his own questions.

Would it always be like this? Jackie wondered. After the Tate case was over and done with (whenever that might be), would Brooks throw himself into the next item of business with the same, almost obsessive determination? One night Jackie woke up suddenly in a sweat, terrified by a dream that her whole life would be like this, Brooks kindly but busy, working until he fell dead. Take it easy, she ordered herself. Remember: The Blade is Brooks's last case. Then comes the campaign for the Senate. The rigours of politics wouldn't be any easier, she knew, but at least she would be able to play a part in the effort. She *couldn't* be left out—wives were an important element in the electoral equation.

Jackie flew to Philadelphia for four days and came away with a firm promise that Aunt Josie would be spending Christmas and New Year in Utah. It was one of those monumental about-faces which Aunt Josie, typically, made seem like a trivial matter. She guessed she would, after all, get on an aeroplane. She was too old to worry about whether or not the machine could actually get her there and back in one piece. Jackie was delighted; promises came hard on the heels of cleanliness, next to Godliness, in her aunt's book.

Sandy was well, as always, back at college for the next academic year, her third. 'You're not missing anything, kid,' she told Jackie on the phone. 'Marianne Carson isn't back this semester, she got married over the summer. And somebody else did. We're all getting the itch to go. Next year will be okay, it's the final year and we'll be coasting. But this year it still looks so far away. It's going to be so slow.'

The Tate trial got under way, and although Brooks was as busy as ever the sheer force of his enthusiasm and excitement rubbed off on Jackie to a certain extent—surprising her in the process. She declined Brooks's invitation to sit in on some of the court sessions, saying she would wait until the trial reached the stage where Tate appeared on the stand to defend himself. For the time being, both sides had a long string of witnesses and experts to parade before the jury.

You're coming to terms, Jackie told herself at one point, and it was at least partly true. She and Brooks would straighten things out between them soon enough. When the trial was over they would lock themselves in the bedroom for several days. In the meantime, she began to exercise a measure of self-discipline, refusing to indulge in any more bouts of anxiety and depression, which she realized were a waste of emotional energy. She saw to her house and the garden, worked out to keep her body trim and supple, read, and began to think about applying to take some university courses on a part-time basis —not so much with a view to eventually achieving a degree, but rather just for the sake of imposing more demands on her mind, and to learn. Jackie noticed that the steadier, more purposeful and self-confident she became, the more responsive Brooks seemed to be. She took it as a sign, small in itself but good, one that indicated she might finally have found the way.

There was only one possible complication, and it seemed so remote that Jackie didn't take it seriously at all. Until the morning of the telephone call. Then she nearly fainted, slumping, dazed, on to a chair.

'Mrs Matthews?'

'Yes.'

'Howdy, this is Doc Adams,' the physician said, putting on his best Milburn Stone imitation. 'I guess, well, no, goldurn it, I know. It's gonna be a baby.'

'Are you—sure?'

'Narrowed it down to either a boy or a girl, or any combination of the two.'

Jackie mumbled thanks and hung up, frustrating a man who had several more authentic lines to render.

No. No. No.

How could it be? Jackie had stored away that morning in a very secret, very private corner of her mind. Without really thinking about it she had decided that it wasn't real, the dream stranger, the fantasy sex. Even when she had missed her period Jackie was sure it was just one of those biological hiccups that occur from time to time. She had gone for a pregnancy test convinced that the result would be negative. Now this.

Fact: Brooks did not make love to her in the last week of July.

Fact: Her period came, right on schedule, at the beginning of August.

Fact: She and Brooks did not have intercourse at all during the month of August.

Fact: The young man appeared on a day in the middle of August. Evidently real.

Fact: She missed her next period and now she was pregnant and there was no way it was Brooks's child.

She had to do something—but what? Could Dr Roger K. Adams fix Jackie and somehow make everything all right, like the wonderful old Doc Adams on *Gunsmoke?* No, Jackie, this is not television, and an abortion isn't quite as simple as having a tooth out. You won't be home in time to shuck the corn and toss the salad. Brooks will have to be told, that's all there is to it.

Possibility: He'll be happy and assume the child is his. (Answer: Don't bet on it; he may be many things but Brooks is not a fool.)

Possibility: If he is suspicious and presses questions, tell him he made love to you in his sleep one night. (Answer: You're not that good a liar, you couldn't get away with it and you'd hate yourself for trying.)

Fact: You hate yourself now anyway. *No.* That was not true. She hated her body now, her body, which was contriving to play some grotesque, ironic trick on her.

Jackie lit a cigarette, puffed a few times, stubbed it out. She couldn't sit still. She put on her sunglasses, grabbed her bag, jumped into the T-bird and tore away from the house, the town.

On the highway Jackie turned the radio up loud. She went south, racing all the way to Provo, where she circled around through the Brigham Young University campus without knowing why and then turned back to the north. Past Cleary Centre, past Salt Lake City, all the way to Ogden. She stopped long enough to have the tank refilled with gasoline and then headed south again. She swung west and drove to Grantsville, where the road ended at the Great Salt Lake Desert. Jackie sat there for a while, smoking, staring out into the barrenness, while the car radio blared absurdly.

East, east, east. She flew as fast as the road would allow, at times pushing the T-bird until it began to vibrate ominously. The Uintas seemed to form a protective wall on her right, blocking off Cleary Centre, Brooks—everything. The rest of the world began to fall away. When she passed Manila she slowed down, somehow feeling distant and safe at last. Jackie turned on to the dirt road to the cottage and stopped. She put her forehead to the steering-wheel and cried, great heaving sobs that ran their course and left her tired, spent. Finally she put the car in gear again and went on to the cottage.

It wasn't hard to come up with a story; Ruth Jenkins accepted it at once. Jackie used the phone to call Brooks and tell him the same thing—that she had left something at the cottage, drove up on sudden impulse, and was now too tired to return until tomorrow. It's so much easier to lie on the telephone.

The cottage felt chilly and unfamiliar, as if it had been stripped of its character and any magic or promise it once might have had. The happy moments Jackie had spent there with Sandy were not even a tiny echo now, and the romantic summer week-ends with Brooks had never come to pass. The air was forlorn as twilight gathered, casting the room in dusky shadows.

Jackie found some gin left in the kitchen and made a drink. She sat down, stretching her legs out on the sofa, and lit another cigarette. She knew that if she didn't pull herself together and see this matter through properly her whole life might begin to fall apart. For the best part of the day she had rattled around the highways and roads of Utah, bouncing from one point to another like a frantic pinball, seeking to avoid something—or find something. Finally she had landed here, taking refuge on the far north-eastern edge of the state. It was no good. She was behaving badly.

There was no getting around it: Brooks would have to be told. It was a dreadful prospect but there were no other real alternatives. Perhaps *he* would demand that she have an abortion. Perhaps he would even throw her out—no, Brooks wouldn't do that, it would make him look like a fool to everyone who knew him. But he might well say that the pregnancy should be aborted, and . . .

Jackie wanted the baby. She knew that, now, with final, immutable certainty. No, she would not be able to live with herself if she agreed to terminate the new life within her. An abortion, even under the best of conditions, still carried the risk of some damage, the possibility that she might never be able to conceive again. Moreover, it would poison and destroy the memory of that morning, the conception, which, however difficult it made her life now, was not something Jackie was willing to surrender. But beyond any such considerations she saw another, simpler truth, and it became the bedrock of her determination. *That's my child, I want to have it, it isn't wrong.*

Persuading Brooks was going to be quite a problem, and Jackie was worried that she might not be able to stand up to him. But he can't force me to have an abortion, he can't knock me out and lay me down on the doctor's table—remember that, remember that his options are limited too.

Jackie reached for another smoke, and then paused. She crushed the cigarette package in her hand and threw it aside. That's got to stop, she decided, I can't poison my child.

She went to bed early, covering herself with extra blankets. Autumn was at hand, the breeze sturdier, sharper, cooler, but she left the windows open because she liked to listen to the sounds of the night.

When it came, Jackie's sleep was deep and dreamless.

The next morning she returned to Salt Lake City. The thought of facing Brooks filled her with fear but the long drive gave Jackie time to nerve herself up for the coming encounter. She parked the car, found a telephone booth and dialled the number of his office. A receptionist connected her without delay.

'Brooks, it's me.'

'Hi, are you back?'

'Yes, I'm in the city now.'

'Good. Everything all right?'

'Brooks, I have to see you. Now.'

'Right now?'

'Yes, it's important.'

'What's it all about? I have—'

'Brooks, I'm your wife. Can't I see you for ten minutes?'

'Sure, but—'

'I said it's important.'

'All right. Do you want to come up here now?'

'No.'

Five minutes later they met on the street corner by

his office. They walked into the park nearby without speaking. Brooks decided to let Jackie start, since she had requested this urgent meeting. They moved slowly along a winding path.

'Brooks, I wanted to see you because I have some news to tell you.'

He nodded but said nothing.

'Brooks, I'm going to . . . have a . . . baby.'

He stopped and turned to her. There was a look of cold hard steel in his eyes. Jackie felt as if she was shrinking, withering away beneath his gaze.

'Whose?' The word like a bullet.

'Brooks, I'm sorry, but you never—'

'I asked you whose baby it is. Who is the father?' Jackie looked away, unable to bear the expression on her husband's face. 'You don't know, you don't even know,' Brooks spat the words out with contempt. 'Jesus fucking Christ.'

'Brooks, I . . .' Jackie was trying, with difficulty, not to cry, but everything she had intended to say just vanished, irrelevant.

Brooks watched her for a moment and then looked into the distance, the muscles in his neck tightening with anger. 'I hope to God that child is going to be white,' he said in a low, menacing voice. 'Because if it's going to be a little chocolate pickaninny or—'

'Don't be ugly,' Jackie flared.

'Oh that's good coming from you. You're my wife, you fuck some other guy, you're going to have his kid, and you tell me not to be ugly.'

'Brooks, you never make love to me any more. What is it, what's happening to us? Don't you want me?'

He started walking again.

'Brooks, I have to know,' Jackie continued, matching his stride. 'You hardly ever touch me. Have you lost all interest, or is there something wrong with me? Do you know how that makes me feel? I didn't want this to happen, but it did. Maybe if you—if we—' The words ran out.

'I wish you hadn't told me this,' Brooks said. 'I wish you'd made some excuse and gone away for a couple of days to get rid of it.'

'I want to have the baby.'

'You *have* to have the baby,' Brooks said, and the words stunned her. 'I've made a few too many goddamn public statements on abortion to be a party to one now and risk having it become known. We'll have the kid and we'll be a family because that's the only way to play it without ruining things completely for me—and I won't let that happen.'

'Brooks—'

'I'm not finished.' He stopped and held her chin between his thumb and first finger, in the manner of a teacher giving a stern warning to a delinquent pupil. 'Don't you ever, ever do anything like this to me again, do you hear?'

'Brooks . . .' The tears started to come. 'We can make it work. Just love me. Like you did. Please. Love me . . .'

NINETEEN

♦

A sullen peace descended on the Matthews household as Brooks and Jackie adjusted to the new situation. They went through the necessary but unpleasant charade of announcing the pregnancy to their friends —and it especially hurt Jackie to have to keep the truth from Sandy and Aunt Josie, but there was no way she could begin to explain the real facts to them. Brooks played the role of a proud father-to-be convincingly, so much so that it unnerved Jackie at times, but her blossoming love for the unborn child carried her through.

Ironically, Brooks began to make love to Jackie again, two or three times a week. But inevitably something was missing, and their sex was mechanical, almost completely joyless. It was as if Brooks believed, consciously or not, that by going through the motions often enough he could eventually bring about a revision of history, that the child would really be his in every way. Jackie was impressed by her husband's show of discipline and acceptance and by his renewed attentions, and if she found it a little sad she was also moved. But her thoughts always returned to the stranger, the real father of her child. Where was he? Would she ever see him again?

In time Jackie came to see what was happening to her marriage. The first few months had been hectic and intensely happy. Then Brooks had allowed himself to be absorbed by his work, leading him to neglect his wife. Jackie, in a moment of weakness, had given herself to a stranger. Pregnancy. Confrontation. Now the dust was settling. Brooks and Jackie were reaching a kind of tacit accommodation. They both had blame to shoulder and the shock might leave scars, but the love between them had not been totally destroyed. Perhaps with time and patience and effort it could be nursed back to health. They were two ordinary, imperfect people who learned a good deal about each other quickly.

Jackie threw herself into the usual activities of an expectant mother—watching her diet carefully, learning a new set of exercises, shopping for the clothes, toys and supplies that would be needed, and pondering names. She began to work on changing one of the bedrooms into a nursery.

One night Brooks had arranged a meeting at the house. Larry Sterling, Mel Dyson and two or three other associates arrived. The trial had reached the point where Jack Tate was about to testify. Brooks wanted to hold a final strategy session to review the case so far and confirm every detail of their plans for handling Tate on the stand. The men gathered together in the living-room. Brooks served a round of drinks and threw another log on the blazing fire. They all sat down, propped long yellow legal pads on their knees and got to work.

Jackie had greeted the visitors and chatted pleasantly with them for a few minutes. Then she went upstairs to paint the baseboard and window trimming in the nursery. It was slow, uncomfortable work, but she didn't mind. The room would look beautiful when the baby came. Brooks had wanted to help, but Jackie insisted on doing all the decorating by herself. She turned on a portable radio and hummed along with the music as she painted.

If marriage was turning out to be quite different from what she had expected, Jackie could at least make sure that her child had a good home and plenty of love. She would make no mistake about that, and she had faith in Brooks. In spite of the low they had been through, she believed that when the time came he would take the child as his own and be a good, loving father. He might still feel hurt inside now and then, even as she would feel wonder and a vague longing when she thought of the stranger, but the child could actually help pull them together. Later, there could be a second child, fathered by Brooks. The healing process would be complete, some day.

As the ten o'clock news came on, Jackie switched off the radio and closed the paint can. She was tired and her back ached. She cleaned the brush in spirits and then went to the bathroom to wash up and prepare for bed. Brooks would probably be up late with his company so Jackie decided to retire with a drink and a magazine. She went downstairs to the kitchen, passing the living-room on the way.

'—like you did Judd Taylor, right?' The voice belonged to the elderly man called Bud, whom Jackie disliked. 'Same sort of thing, exactly.'

Jackie mixed a large but weak drink, spread unsalted butter on a few wheat crackers and went back upstairs.

'Taylor had witnesses that placed him elsewhere, same as this guy,' Bud was holding forth as she passed again. 'But as long as the sonuvabitch wasn't having breakfast with the Pope over in Rome you're all right.'

'Not entirely,' Larry Sterling said.

'Sure you can. Hell, you're too young to remember, but Brooks here nailed Taylor but good, regardless of what this or that witness said. Didn't you?'

Brooks chuckled. 'He stayed nailed too.'

'Damn right,' Bud went on. 'The point is, Tate's got to be cracked on the stand, so the jury can see he doesn't believe his own witnesses.'

Jackie stopped at the top of the stairs, intrigued by what she was hearing.

'I just don't think that's the strongest line,' Larry said. 'If we make too much out of the witnesses, make it look like we're desperate to knock them down, then we might end up giving the jury second thoughts.'

'No, no, no,' Bud scoffed. 'That's his strongest suit, the claim that a couple of people might have seen him other places when this or that murder was being committed. So you have to kill it dead, otherwise, when the jury gets locked away, they'll start brooding on it—and you're lost.'

'But we've already had the witnesses on the stand, and we've cast doubt on their claims. We've established that they saw someone who *might* have looked *like* Tate, but they can't be one hundred per cent positive.'

'Not good enough,' Bud said curtly.

Jackie sat down on the floor at the top of the stairs and sipped her drink. She felt a little like a child snoop, eavesdropping on curious adult talk, fascinated by their serious tones.

'I just think it's a mistake to get off on this when Tate is on the stand,' Larry said. 'I'm not so sure he'll crack for us, and it will only distract from the main thrust of our attack.'

'We can discount the witnesses again when we get to the summation,' Mel offered.

'You're all basically right,' Brooks said impatiently. 'We can go either way. Personally, I want to push Tate on the subject of his witnesses because I think it *will* be easy to trip him up and truss him like a dumb animal. But if it looks like it's not working I can always change tactics quickly enough. But I think he's gettable. I want to have a go. Bud's got a good point. Where Tate was and what he was doing at the times the crimes took place—that's the weakest part of his defence, when you come right down to it. Maybe it's the weakest part of our case too, but that's all the more reason why we have to hammer away at him about it. He'll have to do some monumental lying to hold together all the minor details on those alibis, and that's exactly where we can pick him apart. I've got notes—you wouldn't believe some of the trivia I've compiled, but it's the kind of thing Tate can come unstuck over.'

'But if he sees that coming and simply refuses to fall into it,' Larry said evenly, 'or if he does manage to hold it reasonably together—then we've dug ourselves into a real hole.'

'In the Judd Taylor case,' Bud began, 'the jury probably should have acquitted the guy on this very ground. But Brooks took a chance and turned it around to his advantage. Hell, Taylor had a better witness than the ones this guy's got, but if you work it right, building up a whole lot of small question marks, discrepancies and I-don't-remembers on the side of the defendant, then a jury will often lose sight of a larger, more glaring point against the prosecution.'

'That's right,' Brooks said.

'Fella says he was in a bar having a quiet drink at the time he's accused of being somewhere else breaking the law,' Bud went on. 'Okay, what beer was he drinking? Brand X, he says. Okay, but it turns out that bar doesn't sell X beer. They got U, V, W, Y and Z, but no X. Okay, now he says he must have been mistaken, he must have had one of the others instead. Easy mistake to make, but it's one more seed of doubt to grow in the minds of the jurors. I'm not saying they'll give it any serious thought at all; they don't have to—it's been planted.'

'Yeah, well,' Larry said, sounding bored, as if he had heard this hoary approach years ago in law school.

Jackie rose from her spot at the head of the stairs

and walked into the bedroom. She was puzzled. Settled in bed, she found that she couldn't concentrate on reading her magazine. It may well be insignificant, just a small part of a windy conversation, but it stuck in her mind. 'In the Judd Taylor case the jury probably should have acquitted the guy.' Did he really mean that? Jackie wondered. Brooks hadn't argued or expressed even the slightest reservation. This seemed very odd to Jackie, whose slight knowledge of that old case had given her the impression that it had been a dramatic but clear-cut matter. No questions, no doubts, just the brilliant debut of a bright young prosecutor, Brooks Matthews. So why say 'the jury probably should have acquitted the guy'? It didn't make sense.

Jackie put her magazine down and turned the bedside light off. It was a curious point, and she was sure Brooks could clear it up for her easily—but it might be interesting if she looked into it herself. Yes, if she read up the old reports and newspaper accounts of the trial, familiarizing herself thoroughly with the case, and then went to Brooks with any questions she might have—that would be the way to do it. She ought to know all about the Judd Taylor case anyway, since it was an important event in her husband's life. Brooks might even be surprised and pleased by her interest.

TWENTY

♦

A few days later Jackie went to the court to observe the first appearance of Jack Tate on the witness stand. The room was packed with spectators and journalists, and the air buzzed with anticipation. But as soon as the proceedings got under way the excitement began to diminish. Tate's lawyer led him easily through a well-rehearsed denial of the charges, one by one. The defendant, neat and clean-cut, sporting a crisp new suit, hardly looked like a mass-murderer. His manner was relaxed, almost nonchalant, as if the trial were just a lot of fuss over nothing and would soon blow away. He spoke in a homey drawl and came across as an affable young country boy. Perhaps not overly bright, but then he wasn't being accused of advanced intelligence. And he genuinely seemed incapable of guile or malice. The other people watched with fascination but Jackie began to feel edgy and restless, and she was grateful when the morning session was over.

'He's sure got his "Who me?" act down good,' Larry Sterling said as they adjourned for lunch.

'We'll take care of that soon enough,' Brooks vowed grimly.

Court reconvened at two o'clock and Jackie soon began to feel uneasy again. At first she assumed that the discomfort was due to the fact that she was pregnant, but then another, greater reason dawned on her. It had been building slowly all morning inside of her and now it became clear to her. Jack Tate. His voice. His manner. The way he looked. If he were wearing dusty old denims instead of that suit, if his sandy hair were a little longer and not so carefully combed, he would almost pass for—the stranger whose child Jackie carried.

The blood drained from her face and she felt dizzy. She couldn't sit through any more of this. Jackie made her way awkwardly outside, where she sat down on a bench and slumped over, resting her head in her hands. A guard standing by the courtroom door looked solicitously in her direction but said nothing. He reckoned he'd seen every conceivable show of human distress over his span of years at the courthouse, and he knew when to act and when to stand clear.

Jackie wasn't crying, but she was deeply shaken. She knew it was impossible, that Jack Tate had been locked up in jail and under twenty-four-hour guard the morning the stranger had come to her. But the resemblance was undeniable now that she had recognized it, undeniable and haunting. There was nothing she could do, but it hurt. How many more times will this happen, she wondered disconsolately, how many more times will I see some person who reminds me of him? Someone whose hair or voice or face opens up that memory again, the joy and sorrow, the aching, longing, impossible thoughts . . .

It would happen again that week.

Jackie told Brooks she was sorry but she would have to miss his duel with Jack Tate. Being pregnant made it impossible for her to sit for any length of time in the crowded courtroom without experiencing discomfort. Brooks was understanding about it and each evening he gave her a detailed account of the day's progress in the trial.

Jackie decided to follow up on the idea of satisfying her curiosity about the Judd Taylor case. She could simply go to the public library and dig up the newspaper reports of twenty years ago, but it was easier to start in the study. Brooks would be sure to have his own file on the case, and that in itself might well tell her all she needed to know. If not, then she could go to the library, armed with a precise date and a better notion of what she was looking for.

The study was unmistakably Brooks's room, part office and part male retreat. The large mahogany desk was piled high with books and papers. One wall was covered with photographs, most of which showed Brooks meeting various officials and personalities, shaking hands, raising drinks, always smiling broadly. Four Presidents were there: Kennedy ('With thanks and best wishes'), Johnson ('Best wishes'), Nixon ('Best wishes, as ever, sincerely') and Ford ('From one par 7 to another'). On the top shelf of a bookcase was a lone trophy, dating back nearly forty years to the time when Brooks played Little League baseball. Jackie noticed there were no pictures or obvious mementos of his first two wives. An old radio sat on the small liquor cabinet which Brooks used to hold magazines. A floor lamp stood nearby, and the worn leather armchair that was the only seat in the room besides the swivel-chair at the desk. The thick carpet, like the drapes, was dark brown. Making love here once with Brooks hadn't really changed the atmosphere of the room, Jackie knew.

She turned to the filing cabinets, but when she flipped through the folders grouped under the letter T she could find nothing about Judd Taylor. That seemed odd, but the case could have been filed under some other heading, Jackie thought. Patiently, she started at A and worked through to Z, checking every folder in the six drawers. Nothing at all about the Taylor case.

Jackie sat on the floor, wondering. It looked as if she had made a mistake. Brooks didn't have to keep a file on the Taylor case here at home, however logical it might have seemed to her to assume that he would. The cabinets were full of papers relating to other, less important cases, but that didn't mean anything one way or another. Perhaps Brooks had simply decided to keep all his Taylor material at the office.

The only other possibility was the desk. Jackie stood and stared at it. Looking through the filing cabinets hadn't bothered her, but the desk was somehow a more personal and private domain, one that caused her to hesitate and think again about what she was doing. I'm not being a nosey, snooping wife, Jackie told herself. I'm merely looking for information about an old murder trial. I'm not spying, fishing for anything to hold against my husband. I'll ignore whatever clearly isn't related to the Taylor case.

In the first drawer she pulled open Jackie found a revolver and a small box of bullets, impossible to ignore. Why did Brooks keep a gun in the house, and why hadn't he told her about it? Somewhat taken aback, Jackie nonetheless clung to her resolution and continued searching for anything related to the Judd Taylor case.

She finally found something in the last drawer, bottom left. It wasn't much, certainly not the kind of proper file Jackie had expected Brooks to have. The dusty old manila envelope contained a couple of brittle, yellowed newspaper clippings. She studied them carefully, as if they were the only surviving remnants of a priceless medieval manuscript. Both items were from the same local newspaper on consecutive days in August 1960. The first was fairly brief, reporting that the execution of Judd Taylor in the electric chair would go ahead that day as planned. The

Governor was not expected to order any last-minute stay and his office announced that he was satisfied with the judgement of the last court of appeal, which had turned down a request for commutation of sentence to life in prison. Taylor was said to have given up all hope and resigned himself to his fate. The second was a longer article, conveying dramatically the news that Taylor had been put to death on schedule and recapping the history of the case. This was much more informative, and Jackie sat back, reading it with great interest.

Judd Taylor, age twenty-four, had made something of a name for himself in Utah as a stick-up artist. He was also suspected of committing robberies in Arizona and Colorado, but this was never proven. Taylor mainly hit banks, and he preferred the smaller, poorly guarded branches. He never did organize a major raid for a large sum of money as he considered this too risky. He said he liked 'nice safe snatches', even if it meant that his take was usually not very big. Thus the press and the authorities branded him as a chronic small-timer, which in turn prompted Taylor to begin his own campaign of needling and taunting the police and newspapers. The article Jackie read had to admit that this won Taylor a few fans among the general public. But it quickly added that he was no Robin Hood figure, and that he robbed gas stations, liquor stores and good old Ma-and-Pa groceries whenever he felt like doing so.

There never was a Judd Taylor gang as such. Various people would team up with him to pull off this job or that, and then go their own way, to be replaced by someone else when Taylor needed help. The only person who was permanently involved with him was his girl-friend, Joeline Pangborn, who, on the day of Taylor's execution, was serving a prison sentence of her own for her part in the robberies.

The hunt for Taylor intensified when a bank guard

was shot dead during a hold-up in the town of Emery. The robber wore a mask, which Taylor had never been known to do, but he was the prime suspect. The police, almost accidentally, came upon Taylor and Pangborn asleep in an old line shack in the hills.

The trial had been short and fiery. The state prosecutor was taken ill and his bright young assistant, Brooks Matthews, had to step in at the last minute. He performed brilliantly, winning the case and getting the sentence he wanted: Taylor's death.

The rest of the newspaper clipping provided a few grisly details of the execution. Taylor offered no resistance, but quietly stated for the last time that he was innocent. He had robbed plenty, but he had never hurt anyone. They had to turn the juice on four times for a total of eight minutes before he could be pronounced dead. A couple of the normally hardened prison officials appeared to be quite shaken by what they had witnessed. The smell from the death-house was ferocious.

Well now I know a little more, Jackie thought, but not what I was looking for. The conversation she had overheard a few nights ago strongly suggested that Taylor could have or should have been acquitted. Acquitted. But neither of these articles touched on that possibility. Jackie decided she would go to the public library to see if she could learn more about the trial itself.

As she replaced the two clippings she noticed something at the bottom of the envelope, a piece of paper which she had overlooked before. Jackie took it out and unfolded it. She saw that it was a Salt Lake City Police Department memo, undated, with a few lines of handwriting scrawled in pencil on it.

        KIRK, Edward
        2714 W/Sparrow
        Brigham City

Places Taylor BC.
Reliable/npr

Jackie didn't quite know what to make of it. She was puzzled by the mere fact that a police document was here, in Brooks's study. The handwriting certainly wasn't his. Perhaps one of the police investigators had sent the memo to Brooks. But then if that was what had happened why didn't it have a date, why wasn't it addressed to Brooks, and why was it unsigned and uninitialled?

Jackie refolded the paper, put it back in the manila envelope and returned them to their place in the bottom drawer of the desk. She was no longer sure it had been a good idea to start this little search. She had found a gun with ammunition and a police memo bearing a cryptic message—neither of which she could conveniently discuss with Brooks. She would have to learn more.

The high school student who worked part-time at the library was very helpful. He dug out the right reel of microfilm and put it on the viewer for Jackie. She read through the daily trial reports from beginning to end in one long afternoon.

Brooks had been brilliant, all right. The bank robber had worn a mask, so the state could not produce a witness able to identify Taylor conclusively. The best that could be said was that Taylor was about the same height and build, and had similar hair. Nor could the prosecution come up with the gun that had fired the fatal shot. In spite of these major drawbacks to the case, Brooks pulled it off, trapping Taylor in dozens of minor inconsistencies and lesser admissions that had a cumulative effect on the jury.

Jackie groaned when she saw photographs of Taylor for the first time. They indicated little about his height, weight and hair colour, but they did show his face well. The bone structure, the smile, the boyish grin—all were close enough to make Jackie pause and feel a twinge inside. She tried to convince herself that she was mistaken, that she was reading the stranger's face into others and deliberately haunting herself by using any vague opportunity to justify bringing up his memory again. She forced herself to forget about the stranger and concentrate on Judd Taylor.

In every photograph he appeared smiling and unconcerned. He wore heavy-duty handcuffs that were chained to his leg irons in one picture, but even these encumbrances didn't seem to bother Taylor. The newspaper stories told how he was always joking with the policemen and making witty remarks about some of the people in court.

Jackie came across something which she thought shed light on the note about Edward Kirk. Taylor said that he had been nowhere near Emery at the time the robbery and shooting had taken place, that he had been up in the northern part of the state for that entire month. Because he had been 'laying low' most of the time Taylor could produce no witnesses, aside from his girl-friend, whose testimony was of little value. According to the newspaper Brooks dismissed this flimsy alibi with a snort and a sardonic smile that found company among the members of the jury.

But it made Jackie think. Brigham City was in the north. The police note thus seemed to suggest that someone, Edward Kirk, could place Taylor far from the scene of the crime. The note also said 'Reliable'. But who was Kirk? His name didn't appear once in any of the trial reports in the newspaper, and it surely would have if he had testified. Had Brooks and the police somehow managed to head Kirk off and prevent him from being heard in court? Would Brooks knowingly take part in an effort to suppress important testimony? Would he even give his tacit acceptance to the omission of such testimony? Jackie couldn't believe it, it was impossible, Brooks would never stoop to anything like that, much less send an innocent man to the electric chair. But the pieces of information she was gathering now seemed to point only in that direction, and it made her feel queasy. That feeling worsened when Jackie put on the second reel of microfilm, which covered the time of the execution.

And when Jackie read the sideline article on Joeline Pangborn she hastily turned off the machine and fled the library in anguish and dismay.

TWENTY-ONE

◆

On the front steps of the courthouse Brooks Matthews smiled, shook hands and slapped his colleagues on the back. A small circle of spectators and passersby gathered around him while photographers took pictures and reporters threw out questions.

'Nice work, Brooks,' someone called out.

'You did a good job, Senator,' another person added, arousing some cheers and scattered applause.

Brooks smiled again and shook his head modestly. 'I had a great team and a lot of help,' he said. 'We're all glad it's over now and we can all rest easy in our beds at night, knowing that our wives and daughters are safe once more.'

A local television crew edged in and a microphone was thrust in front of Brooks's face.

'Mr Matthews, is the way now clear for you to declare your candidacy for the United States Senate, as many people expect?'

There were several enthusiastic shouts and some more applause from the crowd.

'I've been giving that some thought,' Brooks admitted to a ripple of amused laughter. 'All I can tell you right now is that when the time comes I won't keep my decision a secret.'

'Are you going to ask for the death penalty when Tate comes up for sentencing?' a pressman asked.

'Absolutely,' Brooks answered promptly, adopting a more serious look. 'The people of Utah have suffered enough already. Too much, far too much. That man went on a rampage up and down our state, terrorizing the entire population, brutally murdering our young women. The people should not now have to foot the bill to keep Jack Tate alive and comfortable in a cosy prison cell for the next forty years or so—much less face the prospect that he might wangle his way out on parole in a few years and be loose on our streets again. So, yes, we certainly will demand the death penalty.' This brought the loudest cheers and applause yet from the crowd.

'What did you think of Tate's defence in court?'

'Non-existent,' Brooks scoffed. 'I thought so all along. I never had any doubt that we would win.' Then he quickly added, 'But I don't want to take anything away from defence counsel—I think he did the best job he could in an impossible situation, and he is to be commended for his efforts. But there's no way you can defend a guilty man.'

'What are you going to do now, Brooks?'

'Get to work on our arguments for the pre-sentencing hearing. It's not over yet, you know.'

The television mike bobbed closer again.

'Mr Matthews, do you think this has been the most important case in your career, which has seen many notable cases over the years?'

'It's hard to compare cases, it really is,' Brooks said. 'But to me this certainly was a very important one. What could be more important, more urgent, than to make sure that our cities and towns, the neighbourhoods in which we all live, are safe, and that our wives and daughters do not live under the threat of meaningless, violent death? It's not often that a lawyer has a chance to work on a case that has such an obvious, immediate impact on the everyday lives of all our people, so, yes, this is one of the most important cases in my career.'

'Do you think you'll get the death penalty for Tate?'

'Yes, but like I said, it's not over yet.'

At the same time, an even larger crowd of people had gathered at the rear of the courthouse. Jack Tate emerged, hands and feet shackled, in a flying wedge of policemen.

'It ain't over,' Tate screamed.

Lights flashed, TV cameras rolled and dozens of questions were shouted out.

'Did you get a fair trial?'

'Fair? What the fuck is fair?' Tate sneered. 'They put on a show and sell it, just what they want everybody to buy, that's all that was.'

'Do you still maintain you're innocent?'

'Mine was not the hand raised to strike down those lives, mine was not the hand.'

Tate's lawyer looked disturbed and said something to him, but Tate shouldered the man aside. For the first time since the trial had begun, Jack Tate was not smiling. His expression was mean and angry. He looked like a man shouting from the crest of a tidal wave as it approached the shore.

'I have heard voices,' he raged.

'What voices?'

'I have heard voices in the night, voices that tell me this is not finished. What will happen when the next one falls?'

'Are you saying that more people will die?'

'Did you hear voices when you killed those girls?'

'Anyone can hear, who has the ears to hear,' Tate replied. 'But no one wants to hear.'

'Are you going to base your appeal on these so-called voices you claim to hear?'

'I will not appeal,' Tate yelled back. 'This is not my court and it's too late for anything now.'

This caused considerable excitement in the crowd. Tate's lawyer looked stricken. 'Get him out of here, get him out of here,' he snarled at the police.

'Did you say you're not going to appeal?'

'I'm not appealing anything,' Tate said. 'It's out of my hands now. No one can stop it or change it.'

The police were trying to hustle Tate into a van nearby but he didn't want to leave yet and the reporters were demanding a few more minutes of questions.

'What do you say to the people who convicted you? The district attorney, the judge and jury—'

'They ought to look at themselves. Let 'em congratulate each other if they think they did the right thing. But they'd better not feel safe because of it.'

'Are you threatening anyone?'

'I don't have to threaten nobody, because they're all in danger anyhow, all the time. Not from me, from themselves, only they don't know it, or at least they act like they don't know it. But some of 'em do, some of 'em do.'

'Do you think all the pre-trial publicity hurt your chances of putting up an adequate defence?'

'Shit, man, you're the ones who put all that out, and now you ask me that? Go fuck yourself.'

'You saw the families of some of the victims in court. Can you look—if they were here now would you be able to look them in the eye and honestly say that you weren't the one who killed their daughters?'

'Could they look me in the eye and honestly say that I am the one who did it? No. If they looked at me, you know what they'd see? Their own hate, their own blindness. I'm just the mirror in this, that's all.'

'You don't feel any regret or guilt about all that's happened? You still maintain you had nothing to do with it?'

'I'm sorry I'm in it, if that's what you mean, but mine was not the hand. The voices say I must ride it out to the end.'

Some of the newsmen groaned and others exchanged smiles, thinking that Tate was stupid to wait until now, after the verdict was in, to come up with this angle of hearing voices. Besides, it was altogether too flimsy to stand up as proof that Tate was a mental case. So why did he persist in bringing up those 'voices'?

'I must see it out,' Tate went on. 'There are others in this and they will follow.'

'Are you saying you had accomplices—one or more?'

'Accomplices?' Tate looked as if he had just heard a foreign word that was incomprehensible to him.

'Ladies and gentlemen,' Tate's lawyer butted in. 'A few moments ago my client said he would not appeal today's verdict. But I would like to assure you that an appeal will be made and—'

'Are you going to change the plea to criminal insanity?'

'I am not insane,' Tate roared. 'I may be the only sane person left here.'

This brought a chorus of open laughter from much of the crowd. Some people started to leave, having heard enough of Jack Tate's meaningless harangue.

'You said this isn't over yet, Jack,' one reporter said as the police were about to thrust their prisoner into the van. 'So as far as you're concerned, what's next?'

Tate looked back over his shoulder at the man who had asked the question. Then it came, the long, chilling laugh that seemed to linger in the air after the van had driven away.

TWENTY-TWO

◆

Early December. Jackie tried to calculate back and recall what she had been doing a year ago. One year and a world past. She and Brooks had been secretly engaged and he had been waging a campaign for a prompt marriage, bombarding her with telephone calls and flying east for intense trysts in New York or Connecticut. It had been a deliriously happy time in her life. Now it seemed an aeon ago. Would she be happier, better off back at college, unmarried, grinding away in a student's life? It didn't matter: that was all gone now. Besides, the past could be illusory too. People always wanted to do something different, to be where they weren't. Precisely those irresistible stirrings had led Jackie to her present situation. *Are there no good choices, no right decisions? What works?*

She heard the car arrive, and then the front door open. Brooks stomped his feet a couple of times and then came into the living-room where Jackie sat, drinking tea. She looked up at him. Snow flurries glistened and began to melt in his hair and on his dark overcoat. His face was rosy from the cold outside, the expression on his face triumphant. In that brief moment Jackie saw again what a splendid-looking man he was, and her heart cried for their marriage, for their love to rekindle itself.

'What do you think?' Brooks said exultantly, as he set down a large brown grocery bag. 'Guilty, guilty, guilty. Three counts of murder one.'

'I'm glad it's over.'

'I know you are.' Brooks bent over and kissed Jackie. 'So am I,' he said. 'Look what I've got.' He turned and pulled two bottles of champagne from the grocery bag. 'For us, now.' He went to get a couple of glasses.

'What was the sentence?' Jackie asked when Brooks came back into the room.

'Oh, he won't be sentenced until February, but it'll probably be death. The judge is pretty much a hardliner and public sentiment is running strong. Rightly so.' The cork popped out and bounced off the ceiling. Brooks poured the champagne. 'Of course there will be an appeal—that's mandatory and automatic in the case of a death sentence. And Tate can lodge his own appeal against the verdict itself, but—' Brooks waved one hand dismissively as if to say that these things were routine and would achieve nothing in the end.

They touched glasses and drank.

'So your big case is over,' Jackie said.

'That's right.' Brooks had settled into an easy chair and now smiled wearily but happily. 'Just the argument for sentence to be made, that's all.'

'Your biggest case ever?'

'In terms of press coverage, I guess so. You can see me on the news on TV tonight. Biggest in a long time, that's for sure.'

'Bigger than the Judd Taylor case?' Brooks was in such a good mood that Jackie decided this might be the right time to raise the subject.

'Different,' Brooks replied, after considering it for a moment. 'Both cases had to do with capital offenses and both got a lot of public attention. But otherwise they're very different matters. Taylor killed one bank guard in the course of a robbery, but Tate has been murdering and mutilating young girls all up and down the state, terrorizing the entire population. So obviously it was a matter of the greatest importance that we get Tate and get him taken care of as soon as possible.'

'But Taylor got the electric chair.'

'Of course.' Brooks sipped his drink. 'He killed a man. Not as part of a regular murder campaign, he wasn't that kind of criminal. But he killed a man all the same, and he paid for it.'

Paying the price meant a lot to Brooks. He used that phrase or variations on it quite often, Jackie noticed. As if everything was part of an enormous equation that provided full redress and balances whenever any part of it was altered or tampered with. The law. Jackie knew that if she argued about it Brooks would patiently tell her that it might not be a perfect system but that it was the best one going.

'You know, since I couldn't sit in court and watch you at work in the Tate trial I decided to expand my knowledge by reading up on the Judd Taylor case.'

Brooks reached to pour some more champagne. 'Really? What on earth for?'

'Oh, curiosity, I guess,' Jackie said. 'Besides, it was the big launching point for your career and a wife should know all about things like that.'

Brooks nodded and smiled thinly. He opened his mouth and then shut it again. Jackie waited. Finally he said, 'It did me some good, but it was just a squalid little shooting by a small-time thug.'

Still calling him small-time twenty years later, Jackie noted. She couldn't tell whether Brooks was reflecting dispassionately on the past or whether in fact he wasn't expressing a note of regret that the crime and criminal that served to establish him as an important young lawyer hadn't been of more significance. You've known him a year now, Jackie chided herself, and you're still not sure how his ego works.

'There are a couple of things I don't understand about the Judd Taylor case,' she said.

'Where did you read about it?'

'Old newspapers at the library.'

'Uh-huh. And what is it you don't understand?' Brooks had a tolerant, paternal expression on his face.

'Well, I'm amazed that he could be found guilty when there was no murder weapon found, and when no one could positively identify him as the bank robber. Whoever did it wore a mask, and apparently that wasn't even Taylor's style.'

'Right,' Brooks admitted coolly. 'You've hit on the two strongest points in his defence. But in fact they're not as strong as they look.'

'Why?'

'Okay. First, it was well known that Taylor did own and carry a gun. He had never fired it in any previous robbery that we know of, but we had plenty of witnesses who could testify that he carried a gun. Now, that gun wasn't found in his possession when he was caught, a fact which adds support to the charge that he killed the bank guard with that weapon. When he had finally used it and realized he might face a murder rap instead of just armed robbery, the first thing he or anyone else in his position would do is get rid of the gun permanently, and fast. I have no doubt that pistol is buried somewhere out in the desert for all time.'

Jackie swirled the champagne in her glass. She had to accept that the explanation was not without plausibility.

'Second,' Brooks continued. 'The fact that he wore a mask doesn't mean anything one way or the other. Most criminals vary their *modus operandi* a little from time to time. Taylor is an example of that, and not just with the mask. Some jobs he had help on, others, like the last one, he pulled by himself. So you can't assume anything from a detail like that.'

'But he couldn't be identified with a mask on,' Jackie protested. 'And the mask wasn't found on him.'

'Naturally not. That would be as devastating as the gun, and he probably ditched it at the same time. As for getting an identification, we established height, build, voice, and maybe even ears—I'm not sure, but I know there was some talk about the ears. Anyway, we had enough.'

'For murder? For the death penalty?'

'Sure,' Brooks said evenly, hitching himself in his chair. He looked as if he was beginning to tire of this line of conversation. 'Especially when we bear in mind the guy's track record. He was bound to have to pull that trigger one day, for sure. Someone sooner or later would try to be a hero and—bang. It's a whole different ball game.'

Jackie looked unconvinced. 'Do you really believe he was guilty, Judd Taylor, of that particular murder?'

'This is getting to be quite a little cross-examination,' Brooks said icily. 'What are you all worked up about anyway?'

'I'm sorry, I don't mean it to sound that way. It's just that I'm trying to—understand.' Jackie felt nervous but determined. *Come on, Brooks, I'm giving you every chance to explain how it was to me. Please, tell me the truth, all of it.* 'Somehow it doesn't seem right or clear to me.'

'Right? Listen, I don't have to believe Taylor was guilty,' Brooks declared, his voice a little louder. 'I *know* he was. We established that in court. I don't see how it could be any clearer.'

'But he said he was innocent, right up to the end.'

'They all do, damn it. You have to look far and wide to find a criminal who doesn't have some reason, some excuse of a story to convince himself that he's not to blame. And Taylor had plenty. Christ, to listen to him you'd think the whole world was going to hell and it wasn't his fault if somebody caught a bullet along the way. He didn't do it. The hell he didn't.'

Jackie looked down for a few seconds. Brooks was getting annoyed, but he wasn't telling her everything about the case. Maybe it didn't occur to him any more. Maybe he had formed a memory of the trial in his mind and it had hardened over the years. But she couldn't stop now. She had to know. It was important: it would tell her something essential about the kind of man she had married, and also, perhaps, about herself.

'You know about Joeline Pangborn,' Jackie said.

'Taylor's girl-friend. What about her?'

'You know what happened to her?'

'She went to jail.'

It's like trying to pull down a wall one brick at a time, Jackie thought.

'You know what happened to her in jail?'

'She—she died, I think.'

'She killed herself. She swallowed ground glass and lye from the prison kitchen, and she stuffed her mouth with bedding in her cell so that no one would hear her screaming that night.'

Brooks had had enough. He put his glass down on the side table and leaned forward in his seat. He pronounced the words slowly, loudly, like someone trying to get through to a foreigner whose understanding of the language was slight.

'Jackie. So what?'

'So what? Brooks, she was pregnant. When Taylor was put to death she killed herself and their unborn child.'

Brooks sat back, holding his temper in check. Now he thought he understood what was going on. Jackie had read up on the Taylor case, taken in some of that garbage about his being innocent and then had come across the facts about the Pangborn girl's death. Being pregnant herself, Jackie had put it all together and worked herself up into a state. It was understandable, the sort of thing a woman would do.

'Jackie, of course that was a terrible thing,' he said soothingly. 'But you have to remember that life isn't all sweetness and light. Those people lived differently. They made their own rules up as they went along, and they knew the kind of risks they were taking. The responsibility rests with them. A lot of terrible things happen in this world but you can't let yourself overreact to them. It doesn't—'

'Brooks, for God's sake don't be so patronizing to me,' Jackie interrupted, her voice trembling with emotion. 'What about Edward Kirk? Who was he? Why didn't he appear at the Taylor trial?'

'What do you know about Kirk?' Brooks hissed, leaping to his feet in a sudden rage, fists clenching at his side. 'I'm the only person who knows about Edward Kirk.'

Jackie was terrified that any second now Brooks would start punching and wouldn't stop until he had beaten her to death.

'He didn't appear because he could have cleared Taylor, right?' Her voice quaked and tears rolled down her cheeks, but she wouldn't stop. 'He was a reliable witness who would have placed Taylor in Brigham City at the time of the shooting in Emery, isn't that so? Isn't it? What happened to Kirk?'

Brooks advanced another step and lashed out with his foot, slamming the second bottle against the hearth, where it exploded, spraying the air with champagne and broken glass. Jackie jumped in her seat at the violence, but made no move to escape. Brooks stood over her, a seething giant.

'You stupid bitch,' he said in a voice low with disgust. 'You stupid, stupid bitch. You have to destroy everything, don't you. Sleeping with another man isn't enough. No, you have to go weaselling around through my desk behind my back and come up with this—this poison.'

'Brooks—'

'You want to know about Edward Kirk? I don't owe

you anything, little girl, but I'll tell you about Edward Kirk. He was a bartender in Brigham City and when the Taylor trial was in the news Kirk phoned the Salt Lake police. Mike Lengyl took the call. Kirk said he thought he could identify Taylor as being a customer in his bar some time during the month the Emery shooting occurred. Mike passed a note to me about it. Three or four days later I called to make an appointment to interview Kirk but I found out he was dead. He was helping a deliveryman unload cases of beer when he keeled over on the spot. Bad heart. That's why Edward Kirk didn't appear at the trial. Maybe he could have said something and maybe not. I doubt it, but nobody will ever know. But one thing everybody does know is that Taylor was the man, regardless of whether he went to Brigham City some time that month or not. Taylor was the one.'

Brooks turned and walked to the fireplace. He leaned one arm on the mantle and poked the remains of the champagne bottle with his shoe. Jackie rubbed her eyes dry, unsure of how much she believed what she had heard. It was plausible, like so much of what Brooks said, and it would be easy for her to check on the circumstances of Kirk's death. But how could Brooks be so sure that Taylor was guilty? That was what gnawed at her. He *couldn't* be that sure, no matter what he said. And every one of his explanations, however reasonable, had the perverse effect of strengthening her doubts. Maybe she was wrong, maybe she was making nonsense of the facts—but Jackie didn't think so. She was certain that Judd Taylor and Joeline Pangborn were the victims of a terrible mistake twenty years ago.

'As soon as we're into the New Year,' Brooks said, 'the campaign will start. Unofficially at first, of course, but it'll start all the same. I can't have you stirring up shit and making life difficult, do you understand?'

Jackie closed her eyes and nodded. Typical Brooks,

hard and practical, planning the next step.

'I've tried,' he went on. 'After what happened before, I have tried to make things work and to make them good. But I can't do it alone. You have to play your part, whether you like it or not. Do you understand?'

Jackie nodded again. She knew her part: the smiling, silent, uncomplaining wife of the illustrious candidate. Had she ever imagined she might have a real role to play, a serious contribution to make to a campaign of issues and ideas? Not any more. Now she had no doubts about what it would be like with Brooks. His whole universe was just an extension of himself and his certainties. Jackie was a part of it, yes—like a possession acquired to serve a specific purpose.

Brooks continued talking, but Jackie only half-listened to what he said. He can't reach me any more, she realized, and I can't reach him. It was a mistake. She had fallen, and fallen gladly, for a father-figure, an illusion that had promised to heal an ancient wound in her life and meet her needs. But she had been wrong. And now there was nothing she could do about it. He wouldn't get rid of her, he couldn't let her go. They were locked together . . .

. . . While somewhere out there, she knew, there was another man, younger, more alive to her still, the man who was her real lover and the real father of her child.

'Are you listening to me?' Brooks asked, startling her. 'I try to talk to you and you're off in a daydream.'

Jackie turned to him.

'You know what you are, Brooks,' she said. 'You're a shit.'

She left the room.

TWENTY-THREE

♦

The long winter months dragged by, the slow grind of nature's hardest season. Brooks and Jackie staggered on together, like two people who could do nothing but cede themselves to form and routine. They did what married people do: ate together, slept together, went out together, coped . . . But it was a concussed marriage and the only thing they were both reconciled to was having to live with each other. Jackie despised Brooks for the cynical ease with which he performed the part of a happy husband and father-to-be, and she despised herself for going along with it. All affection and joy were gone, and whenever Brooks touched her, forced her to satisfy him one way or another, Jackie felt invaded and used. But she had neither the power nor the will to resist.

As long as the roads were clear of snow Jackie managed to escape for a few hours each day and find some sense of freedom in her car. She drove in all directions, aimlessly, with no destination in mind. Sometimes, when she spotted a hitch-hiker in the distance ahead, her heart would give a quick leap in foolish anticipation—but it was never the right person.

Aunt Josie, as good as her word, arrived a few days before Christmas, pronouncing air travel noisy and unpleasant, but a useful form of penance. She cheered up Jackie quite considerably just by being there, and the duration of her visit was the one bright spot in the entire winter. Brooks was typically jolly and charming with the old woman, giving an airtight performance of a model husband and all-around wonderful guy. As far as Jackie was concerned this Christmas was Aunt Josie's, and she didn't let her feelings towards Brooks show, even when he was being so unctuous she wanted to vomit.

Christmas Day and the opening of presents passed easily with glasses of Brandy Alexander. Jackie couldn't avoid the temptation to give Brooks one 'joke' gift: an electric roll of toilet paper that would unwind itself when switched on. He laughed dutifully.

New Year's Day, also being their first wedding anniversary, was more of a strain. Twice Jackie retreated to the bathroom where she sat feeling miserable and loathsome. It seemed a cruelly apt summary of the current state of her life that she was reduced to participating in an elaborate lie to Aunt Josie, a woman for whom she felt only love and respect and gratitude. Somehow she got through the day and the toasts at dinner.

Aunt Josie left on 3 January. Jackie drove her to the airport and they had time, before the flight was called, for a cup of coffee. After a few minutes of idle chat Aunt Josie squeezed Jackie's hand.

'It'll be better,' she said comfortingly. 'I can tell it's hard on you now, isn't it?'

Jackie nodded. 'A little.' Of course Aunt Josie had noticed something; Aunt Josie always noticed.

'I know, it's like that sometimes, worse when a body's with child. And the holidays don't help, with all that bother and rushing around to get things done. But it'll be better.'

Jackie smiled wanly. 'I hope so. I do get tired and depressed, and I don't know what to do with myself half the time.'

'Of course you get tired, and you feel big and clumsy carrying that baby around inside you. But you take care of yourself and everything'll be all right, you'll see.'

Aunt Josie was right about most things, but this time Jackie wasn't sure. The weeks, the months —seemed to be endless obstacles between her and some unknown future. Was there any future at all, she wondered, or was this it—one enormous boulder-like block of time piled on another, and another, beyond counting?

Jackie drove and drove, until she thought she must know every road in the state by heart. And still she drove, always falling back, tired and drained, to Cleary Centre and her house, the inescapable point of gravity that claimed her.

There were times when she would be sitting reading or watching television and suddenly she would burst into tears, crying uncontrollably until she passed into sleep. Then Jackie would awaken an hour or so later sticky with sweat, her clothes feeling like some horrid second skin. She would go to wash and change, and then catch sight of herself in the mirror—eyes puffy, face blotchy, hair dank and tangled, everything about her adding up to a wretched, ugly mess. And she would want to scream and cry again, but there was nothing left inside. Until the next time.

Brooks continued to play his part with functional efficiency. He was helpful and considerate of Jackie's condition, taking on most of the day-to-day household chores himself. There was something grim and soulless about it all, Jackie knew, but she was grateful for the help.

In April Jackie sat down and gathered together a small pile of notes and photocopies. Months ago she had worked on all this Judd Taylor material, old newspaper clippings, the memo from Brooks's desk and her own unfinished attempt to set the story down on paper as it appeared to her. Now it didn't seem to mean anything. Just a foolish exercise born of a sudden, passing impulse. One more item lost somewhere along the way. Jackie wanted to tidy it up, to dispose of it one way or another, but she was reluctant simply to destroy it. She put the papers in a clean manila envelope (it had started with one, why not end with one?), sealed it and wrote her own name on the front with a black felt-tip pen.

Now, what to do with it. After a moment's thought Jackie took a few sheets of blank paper and began to write. The words formed a jerky, off-centre network across the page.

Dear Sandy,

Please stash away the enclosed some place safe and keep it for me. It's nothing too important but I'd be most grateful if you would oblige. Someday I'll ask for it back, or if I forget you can remind me when you reach graduation next year. If anything should happen to me, all you have to do is burn it—after reading it, if you want.

Things aren't so good here. I feel like I'm caught up in something beyond my control, like a piece of driftwood carried on the tide. Who knows where? Is that pregnancy or is it just me? I don't know, but I hope it changes for the better next month when the baby is due. It's been a long nine months, let's hope it was worth it. Pregnancy is supposed to be a wonderful time, but you reach a point where it seems impossible to go on and you say to yourself, this is far enough, come on, let's get it over with now. Am I putting you off the whole idea? Sorry, ask me again what it was like in a few months.

Brooks is his usual self. Did I tell you the final result of that big Tate trial he was handling? The guy was given the death sentence and he surprised everybody by waiving his right to appeal. An appeal was filed anyway, that's normal procedure, but it was turned down a couple of weeks ago. Looks like he'll get his wish before too long.

Brooks is really into the political thing now, lining up his supporters, planning and replanning every minute of the campaign up to election day in November. Looks good, one private poll has him out front at the moment. But it holds no great attraction for me. I'll have to make a lot of appearances with him, and I'll have the baby to take care of.

I'd love it if you could get out here again this summer for a while. A chance for you to see what motherhood involves. And we could get away to the cottage at the lake. Please, please.

That's it, I have to go lie down for a while. Doing anything, even sitting still, makes you tired and a little crazy when you're at this stage.

Love,
J.

The last weeks became even more difficult to bear as Jackie was no longer able to drive even short distances comfortably. She was virtually housebound, and feeling as big as a house herself. She watched television all day, every day, until it seemed her brain was fried to a cinder. Sometimes she would go and sit in the nursery for a while, the pretty, fresh room she had finished herself. To her it was the most peaceful room in the house, a colourful miniworld just for children. If only she could lie down there to sleep and then, magically, wake up a three-year-old child again, before...

Justin Pierce Matthews was born nearly three weeks early, small but in good health. Jackie cried with joy. After months of increasing struggle, the birth had been surprisingly fast and uncomplicated.

'Y'see, the way I figger it,' Doc Adams said, arms folded across his chest, 'that boy just wanted to git out here quick as he could and see fer himself what it's all about. Nuthin' wrong with him, no-sir. Curious's all.'

The baby had blond, downy hair and bright eyes, and he gained weight steadily. Jackie was sure she could see the father in the boy's face, and now the sensation didn't bother her. On the contrary, it finally seemed right and good, and she spent long hours just watching the infant, holding him close and letting her mind wander to thoughts of that long-vanished person.

He had come to her to give her only love, to make an oasis of delight out of one morning in her life. Now he was the only man Jackie felt she might be able to say she loved, in a way. He was gone, but a part of him lived on, in her child, as well as in her heart. The child of a dream, the only dream she had left.

Jackie had delivered not only a baby boy, but also herself—to some new point in her life. The clouds and turbulence of the past year and a half fell away and now were eclipsed completely. She had arrived at the next shore, with a son, and if she was a little unsure she was at the same time open and ready for whatever she might find. She had Justin now and with him she could find the strength and the way to build a new world for herself from the inside out. A world in which she would find her own peace.

4
REUNION

TWENTY-FOUR

◆

Close up, they were dingy grey, massive, forbidding, squat-looking in spite of their height, barren, solid and silent as a tomb. They were repellant, even miles away they were repellant. Why, then, was she drawn to them now?

One day, driving around aimlessly, Jackie had found herself close to the prison walls. Rabar—the word itself was hideous. But she sat in her car staring at the place for nearly an hour. After that, again and again, as today, her route always seemed to bring her this way.

Justin, strapped into his special car seat in the back, sneezed, spitting out his pacifier. Then his eyes fluttered shut and he was asleep again. Sometimes Jackie spoke in a dreamy voice to the child, but mostly she sat, watching the walls.

He was in there. Jack Tate. Oh, he wasn't the man, though to look at him he almost could be. No, he was an echo, a reminder, a shadow of . . . her vanished lover and Justin's true father. Perhaps that was why she returned here again and again, to be close to an image, a likeness, even if she couldn't see him.

It's a foolish obsession, she told herself more than once. But she couldn't stay away. Jack Tate meant something to her, in a way that eluded her full understanding. The impulse rang true. Jackie felt almost kindly towards the man. He was going to play an important part in her life, although she didn't know exactly what or how. A sacrifice, a gift—something. Did he know it? She wondered if he had any idea. She would like to have the chance to meet Tate. It would never happen, but she imagined what it would be like. All she could say to him was, 'Thank you.'

'Smoke?' The guard held an open pack of Camels to the bars of the cell.

'No thanks,' Jack Tate said.

'How you doing?'

'Okay.'

'You'll be here for ever, don't worry.' It was as close to comforting as the guard could manage to sound.

'You think so?'

'Sure, they'll argue for years, bouncing the ball back and forth. They hate to be the ones to decide.'

'That's funny,' Tate said. 'I have the feeling they're all eager to get on with it in this case.'

'Nah, you'll see I'm right.'

'I don't really care,' Tate said evenly.

'Say, Jack, tell me something, would you? Did you really off all them girls?'

Tate smiled. 'What do you think?'

'Me? I don't know. They got you for three of them . . .'

'And?'

'Well, me and some of the other guards were wondering. How many were there altogether?'

A hollow laugh came from the prisoner. 'You want a body count,' he said. 'Is that it? How many did I really kill?'

'Hey, it don't mean nothing to me, Jack. Just

curious, that's all. It's not, like, personal, you know.'

'Of course not.' Tate laughed to himself again and shook his head. 'What can I tell you? Ten? Thirty?'

'Thirty? Jesus!'

'There are no numbers,' Tate continued. 'There are only bodies, bodies everywhere. More than you know, more than anyone knows. Bodies, so many bodies, more even than I know. Lost, lost, and they'll never be found, you know. Never. All over the place . . .'

'Aw, come on, Jack.'

'If I could do a list, or draw a map of where they all are, it would be—'

'Do you want paper and a map?' The guard suddenly thought he might be on to something.

'It would be no good. The count hasn't ended yet. Maybe it never will.' Tate looked up. 'I can't find them all, you know.'

'It's not a big house,' Jackie whispered. 'Not as big as this one. But it's the right size. It fits, and we fit in it. Is it a cabin? I don't know. Maybe. Or a small ranch. It's just a good, honest house. With clean windows and a good view that you want to look at, and land that's used for something. We grow all kinds of food—corn, tomatoes, carrots, squash, beans, lettuce and strawberries—lots of strawberries. And we have our own animals too. Chickens that give us eggs every day, and a cow for milk. Rabbits, maybe even a goat. And of course a dog; we must have a dog. What kind of dog would you like?

'No, we won't be alone. Daddy is with us all the time, because he has to take care of the garden and the animals we're raising, and he doesn't have to go away every day. Not any day. He's always right there, where we need him. He'll teach you all kinds of things. How to fish, how to find things in the woods. How to look after yourself. He'll teach you everything, don't worry about that. There isn't anything Daddy can't take care of.

'Do you love him as much as I do? Of course you do. He's never lied to us. He's never hurt us. He's not cold or mean or too busy for us. He has all the time in the world for us, all the time in the world. You'll see. And if you ask him, he'll tell you the name of every star in the sky.

'I don't know where the house is. That's the surprise. That's what we're waiting for. But I know it's far away from here and in a beautiful place. That's what he's doing now, finding it and getting it ready for us. It has to be just right, you know. Good, sweet water from our own well that goes down deep into the earth. Good soil and light. And the house, a good, honest house that we can live in like it's a part of us. Only Daddy can find it all for us. And when he does, he'll take us there.'

Jackie smiled sadly. She sat up and checked the crib. Justin was asleep.

'Wasn't that a nice story?'

'You weren't even listening tonight.'

'To what?' Brooks asked indifferently.

'To Justin. He's trying to speak now. He says words. He was trying to say something to you at the dinner table, and you weren't even listening.'

Brooks shrugged. 'Babytalk.'

'No it wasn't,' Jackie insisted angrily. 'He was trying to speak words. If you paid him any attention at all, you'd hear for yourself.'

'Cut it out, Jackie.'

'Cut it out? You can't even look at the child for one lousy minute? Is that what you mean? You can't even do that?'

'Don't give me that.'

'I'm asking too much of you again. Right?'

'Sometimes you can be a real pain in the butt, Jackie. You know that?'

'I've learned not to expect much from you, Brooks, but the way you treat Justin, ignoring him all the time, acting as if he didn't exist—that really says something about you.'

'That I won't play the cute little game of happy Daddy? You're damn right. We do what we have to do in public, Jackie, but I don't have to lie to myself in my own home.'

'Lie to yourself? What does that mean? A child—a baby tries to speak to you and you can't even listen. Now you try to dignify that kind of behaviour by—'

Brooks rose from his chair and crossed the room to pour himself a large, neat whisky.

'So he walks away again.'

Brooks turned and looked at her. 'I haven't walked away,' he said, restraining his anger. 'It should be pretty damn obvious that I haven't walked away from anything, in spite of having all the reason in the world for doing so.'

'I can understand—even after all this time, Brooks —I can understand your attitude towards me. You can feel that way, you can punish me for the rest of my life if that's the kind of person you are. But why do you have to be that way with Justin? He's never done you any harm, he's just a helpless, innocent child. Are you going to punish him for ever too?'

'*His* child,' Brooks snarled.

'Is that what's eating you up inside?' Jackie asked quietly.

Brooks didn't answer.

A brief shower had come and gone, but the light rain did nothing to improve the appearance of the prison. Rabar glistened like an evil slug of monstrous proportions. Jackie sat in her car, unable to take her eyes off the place. She held one hand, clenched tightly in a fist, pressed to her heart.

Aunt Charlotte, I've made a mess of it. Such an awful mess. What can I do? How can I save my son and myself from this—this life we're trapped in? What would you do?

Aunt Charlotte, will he ever come back? Will I see him again? Will his son ever know him? Would you search for him? Where? I've looked and looked, and cried and cried.

How many mistakes can a person make, and still carry on? I can't love Brooks. I never did. He was a fantasy that ended as soon as I tried to make it real. I can't live with him. But if I leave, where can I go? There is no home. I would just be running. I can't stay, I can't go. What will happen to my son?

Jackie opened her hand and stared at the locket she held, the one Aunt Josie had given her on the day of the wedding. The faded grey picture of Aunt Charlotte offered no answers. Aunt Charlotte, who, as a teenager, had run away with a much older man, and surprised everyone by living happily. Ever after? A lifetime. What more could anyone ask?

But you can't help me now. You're a ghost.
Like the one I love.

TWENTY-FIVE

◆

The day broke dark and humid. There wasn't the slightest trace of a breeze to move the air and it was obvious to anyone who bothered getting out of bed that by noon the town of Cleary Centre would be stewing in a pressure cooker formed by the hard-baked earth and the low, slate-grey sky. On days like this people wake up feeling more tired than when they went to bed, but still they rise to the unhappy prospect and go sluggishly, leadenly about their business.

Brooks showered early and ate a quick breakfast of toast and coffee. Jackie sat at the table, sipping cold orange juice and feeding cereal to Justin a spoonful at a time. The heat made the child cranky and uncomfortable. Brooks had put air-conditioners in the nursery and the master bedroom, but somehow they weren't enough. The stifling, debilitating heat still seemed to get through, if only psychologically.

'Big day today,' Brooks said, flipping through the morning newspaper. 'After this, the campaign goes public and the race is officially on.' He looked pleased.

Jackie saw the front-page headline. BLADE TO FRY it proclaimed in ghoulish tabloid triumph. And then the subhead: 'Tate Gets Electric Chair Today in Utah Heatwave.' What bad taste, Jackie thought. But she felt her own secret thrill of anticipation.

'Is there any chance he might get a last-minute stay of execution?' she asked.

Brooks chuckled. 'Are you kidding? If we called for volunteers we'd have a few thousand people down at the prison in no time, ready and eager to throw the switch. I don't think you could find anyone in the whole state who'd be willing to go out on a limb and say the guy should live. Not after the things he's done. Nothing can save Jack Tate today, that's for sure.'

Jackie grimaced. Brooks was looking forward to the victory celebration. He was like a man whose team was ahead by thirty points with only a minute to go in the game. The other side had no time-outs left.

For the past week the press and media had been carefully building up an atmosphere of ugly, morbid anticipation. Tate had refused to take part in any appeals on his behalf and even the Supreme Court had declined to block his execution. Jackie remembered part of one interview that had appeared in a newspaper.

'It'll happen again if it isn't finished now,' Tate told the reporter.

'Do you mean that if you don't go to the electric chair now you will get out of prison some day and perhaps kill again?'

'I didn't say that. I just said that it'll happen again if it isn't finished now.'

'What do you mean by that?'

'Just what I said.'

'Mr Tate, if this is what you want—'

'Yes sir, it is.'

'Why, then, did you not plead guilty in court? Why did you try to defend yourself?'

'Okay, there's a couple of things here. One is, I'm not the one guilty, that's what I think. I mean, we're all responsible, but guilt is another matter. I still don't feel guilt for any of this. But the other part is, I knew they was goin' to find me guilty anyhow. No matter what. Now, I could have saved them a lot of time and effort and money by pleading guilty, but if I did that there was a danger they might get to feelin' generous and would decide just to lock me up for life. Maybe in a padded cell. I couldn't take that. I live for my freedom, man. Well, leastwise this way it'll all be over for good, and I can face that. I may not like it, but I can face it.'

Brooks disturbed her thoughts by kissing Jackie perfunctorily on the cheek, making a face at Justin and then turning to leave.

'See you this evening,' he said.

'Goodbye, Brooks.'

The door closed.

'Do you want more cereal, honey?'

'No.' Although Justin's vocabulary was still rather limited, this was one of his favourite words and he never hesitated to use it firmly whenever there was something he didn't like.

'Do you want some milk?'

'No.'

'Orange juice?'

'No.'

'Do you want anything, honey?'

'No.'

Jackie carried the child into the living-room and set him down in the playpen. Justin whimpered but didn't resist. Jackie turned on the television set and found cartoons on one channel.

'Just for a few minutes, honey, while Mummy goes upstairs. Look, there's Hong Kong Phooey.' Poor child, she thought. So dependent and so harmless. Yet so easily harmed. Don't worry, little one, it will be all right. Soon, soon.

Should she phone Aunt Josie and Sandy? No, it was too early in the day back East. Besides, there would be time later for them to understand.

Jackie was sorry that Sandy had been unable to visit her again this summer. But she had found a good job for ten weeks, needed the money and simply couldn't get away. I might have been able to explain it to her at the lake, Jackie mused. The lake. Jackie remembered the day she had stumbled across that gravestone in the middle of the woods. How she had worked on it until the letter Z came clear. Yes, I remember you, whoever you were, out there alone, at one with the earth. Somebody still knows a little about you. Where you came to rest.

It would be harder on Aunt Josie, that was certain. It was the kind of thing that could only be explained to her in person, face to face. But that was impossible now. Jackie reminded herself that Aunt Josie was a resilient woman, a woman of character and fortitude. In time, in time . . .

Jackie looked at Justin again. She smiled. Yes, it will be all right. Everything will be all right. How do I know? Because, my darling son, it has to do with dreams and memories and love and destiny, things like that, all moving as slowly but irresistibly as continents. Together, apart, changes so fine we hardly know they've taken place, until after.

That's how the knowledge had come to her —gradually, over a period of weeks. When did it all begin? Around the time Justin was born. At some point the knowledge, the certainty nudged its way into her conscious mind, and there it blossomed. Impossible to believe, impossible to deny.

Jackie glanced at the clock. Nine forty. She went to the front screen door and looked up and down the street. Other houses were fat rocks in the distance. The road, a soft and spongy ribbon. The trees hung limply, waiting for the end of August and the first lick of a breeze. And here, almost at her feet: an expanse of burnt lawn that marked a place where people lived. Unreal, oh unreal.

Jackie went to the kitchen and poured a large glass

of iced tea to take upstairs. She had to get ready.

Brooks—what about Brooks? Too bad, Jackie thought. There was nothing she could do for him any more. He was caught in his own life, and maybe it was even good for him. But for Jackie, and for her son, it was nothing more than a trap. They had to break free, and now she knew the way. Brooks would survive it all, Jackie was sure. He's the kind of person who can turn any eventuality to his advantage somehow.

Thank you, Brooks. You came into my life and made it yours. For a while. It wasn't all bad and I did love you once, but it hasn't worked. I'm getting out of your life now, and I'm taking my child with me. Thanks for—whatever it was.

Jackie removed her nightgown and went into the bathroom to wash. She scrubbed her face, her teeth, and then she brushed her long hair until it was silky and smooth. She loved the feel of it on her bare shoulders and back. Swept forward, it almost covered her full breasts. Yes, you do have a beautiful body, she told herself, even after giving birth, and even if Brooks hardly ever noticed. Ah, but someone else will.

Back in the bedroom Jackie sorted through her clothes. There was plenty to choose from, but she knew exactly what she wanted: the pretty, off-white, three-quarter-length dress she had worn only once before, back at school. She put on a bra and then her best stockings, topped with garters on her thighs. She wanted *him* to be able to reach up under her dress and touch *her,* not panty hose. The dress was a trifle snug in the bust, but otherwise it fitted comfortably enough.

Jackie sat down in front of the mirror and applied some light make-up to her face. You look good, she thought, you really do look good. Like a young girl on the verge of womanhood, poised to step forward into the new and the wonderful. Once the tide pulled, the movement began, nothing could prevent the flow of things from running its course. The trick was to see what it was all about in the first place, and then to go with it and ride it all the way.

The clock showed 10.43. Jackie looked out of the bedroom window. The sky was blacker now. Along the road far below, the front porch lights of many houses were turned on. Waiting for the big moment. People are sick, Jackie thought. It's like a public holiday or a big carnival to them, the way they deliberately put their lights on just to watch them flicker when the electric chair is used today.

On the distant hilltop: Rabar Penitentiary. The ugly grey spot sat like an oily fungus on the land. But Jackie had long since ceased to hate the sight of the place. In fact, it had become a necessary part of her life. She could understand that now and she almost felt grateful for it. Today Rabar would perform its last service for her, and then she would never have to look at it again.

The way out, the way out, Jackie's found the way out, the words danced through her mind like a child's song. Yes, she knew the way out now. She wouldn't be surprised this time. She hadn't taken sleeping-pills in weeks—she wanted all her senses to be awake and alert when the time came. She would be ready.

Jackie turned to the full-length mirror on the closet door and examined herself again. Yes, she looked right. She closed her eyes for a moment and imagined once more the feel of his hands on her body. The excitement grew in her. It was today. Soon. Now and for ever.

He would come.

He would come for her.

He would come for her and their child.

Then they would drive, drive through the day and into the night, through the mountains, past lakes, across deserts and plains, streaking through ramshackle towns and forgotten junctions, racing across the open empty land beneath the Big Sky, driving to

Texas or Mexico, or north to Canada or west to California, or even to the Sandhills of Oklahoma—it didn't matter where. They would all three be together at last, driving away from all the smog and into themselves...

Jackie didn't know how or why, but she knew beyond a doubt that her lover, the dream stranger, would return for her and Justin today, as sure as the shockwaves that would soon emanate from Rabar to blink out a whole town for a couple of minutes. Then—freedom.

'No.'

Jackie turned, remembering Justin. He must be fed up stuck in that playpen, she thought. Don't worry, dear one. We're going soon. Very soon.

The chandelier downstairs began to chime.

Jackie spun around and looked at the clock-radio. Its illuminated red face flashed and dimmed, flashed and dimmed in a coruscating frenzy.

Now.
He's here.
Now.

Leaving the air-conditioned bedroom was like stepping into a furnace and walking across deep sand dunes, the air so thick but dead you could almost drown in it.

The chandelier continued to make its music, which seemed to float up like tiny bubbles from a great depth. Jackie moved down the stairs. Outside, she knew, porch lights were flaring and dying all over town.

The living-room was dark, shades drawn.

A wall of heat held her briefly at the entrance.

Then accepted her.

She saw Justin on the far side of the room. He was sitting on the floor, at the feet of the young man.

The dream, the dream. Yes, here I am, she wanted to say. I've waited for you with our son, so long, so very long, but I knew you would return. You said you would, and we waited. Now, here we are. Take us away from this place.

The young man looked up at her and smiled. His lips moved but made no sound. Jackie reached out to him. Suddenly he seemed to be upset. His eyes narrowed and his mouth moved angrily. Strange, incoherent sounds blurted into her mind and then were swallowed by silence before she could understand them. There was a look of anguish and unfathomable rage in his eyes.

He stood up and there was something very wrong in his smile. He looked at the child and Jackie followed his gaze. Now she saw dark blotches on the carpet. Justin wasn't moving. His face was purplish black. His mouth and nostrils were stuffed with cotton wadding. Then the young man nudged the child with his dusty boot. Justin's head slid off his shoulders and on to his lap.

Jackie's legs buckled and her arms fanned the heavy air helplessly. She screamed and screamed inside, but no sound came from her.

Her lover was moving across the room towards her. The look on his face was evil and malignant. He was laughing the noise of shrill static—it seemed to slash through her ears to the centre of her brain. Then he was inches away, laughing, roaring in her face, searing her skin with hot, foul breath. So close, his features were overwhelming. Teeth like gravestones, pores like craters—he was a sea of shape and form, slipping in and out of focus.

Judd Taylor, dead more than twenty years? Jack Tate, dying in the electric chair a few miles away from here? The real Blade, still free? Her one true lover, returned for—this? Jackie tried to understand what was happening but her mind was filled with horror. He is not Judd Taylor, that can't be. He is not Jack Tate, that can't be. *He is not my lover because I've been in love with a ghost, a dream* ... The young stranger seemed to be two or three or four figures in one, layered, interfacing, coming together—reaching for her.

The Blade.

The sickening laughter.

Then the hunting-knife became a long arc of silver fire that tore Jackie free of herself and sent her flying after Justin into the dreamless dark.

EPILOGUE

◆

Salt Lake City (6 Feb.). Tragedy again struck prominent Utah attorney Brooks Matthews when he suffered a severe heart attack yesterday afternoon. He is expected to survive but he remains on the critical list and a hospital spokesman confirms that there are indications of permanent paralysis. Matthews, 49, made an unsuccessful bid for the Senate in last November's elections, after the shock of . . .